Tuppney's Tales

To Linda
Love
Joyce x

JA Cooper

To Linda
Love
Peter x

A Cooper

Tuppney's Tales

Joyce Annie Cooper

Date of Publication:

Published by:
J A Edwards
50 Paddock Heights
Twyford
Berkshire
RG10 0AR

Cover illustration by Claire Broomby

Printed by:
ProPrint
Riverside Cottage
Great North Road
Stibbington
Peterborough PE8 6LR

ISBN: 0 9543472 0 X

CONTENTS

Chapter One
Lindrick   1

Chapter Two
Sunderland Street   9

Chapter Three
The Gypsies   17

Chapter Four
War   21

Chapter Five
Bath Night   27

Chapter Six
Sunday School   31

Chapter Seven
Our Dad   35

Chapter Eight
Infant School   41

Chapter Nine
Christmas   47

Chapter Ten
Scarborough   53

Chapter Eleven
Millie's Wedding   55

Chapter Twelve
Castlegate   61

Chapter Thirteen
Moving In   69

Chapter Fourteen
The Shop   77

Chapter Fifteen
Junior School   83

Chapter Sixteen
Playtime   89

Chapter Seventeen
Water Lane   101

Chapter Eighteen
Pets   109

Chapter Nineteen
Winter's Evening   117

Chapter Twenty
Babies   125

Chapter Twenty-one
Senior School   131

Chapter Twenty-two
Helping Our Mam   141

Chapter Twenty-three
Dad   151

Chapter Twenty-four
Pantomime/Tanner Hop   155

ACKNOWLEDGEMENTS

To Doreen, Enid and Lionel, my ever loving sisters and brother for jogging my memory and answering my endless questions.

My dear friend Bett Davenport, who patiently read and reread my tales, laughing and crying along the way with me.

And for my John especially, for believing in me.

With all my love.

DEDICATION

This is for Amie, my grand-daughter, when she comes to stay she always climbs into bed with me in the mornings and I tell her about my childhood and we laugh and giggle at the things I seem to remember when I am with her. You see she reminds me of me when I was a child.

CHAPTER ONE

LINDRICK

My name: Joyce Annie Cooper.

I was born on 23rd November 1936 at Lindrick Cottage in a small farming village in South Yorkshire called Tickhill. Looking back I had an idyllic childhood but it's only when you grow older that you realise it.

There were four of us, Lionel, he's my brother, he's four years older than me, then comes Doreen one year after our Lionel and I arrive one and a half years after Doreen, then came our Enid, she's the baby of the family and arrived one year and four months after me. We were to find out later that we had another sister and brother but they were older and didn't count in our happy little world at Lindrick.

Tickhill at that time was a small village with twelve farms, eight public houses and one working man's club.

The village is set around the eighteenth century Butter Cross, a large grey stone dome with four steps all the way round leading up to the flag stone floor, with eight large round pillars that we couldn't get our arms around holding up the dome and right on the very top is a big, ornate, metal weather vane with a beautiful arrow on, there is a pump trough which has a drinking cup on a chain standing just beside. It has a Parish Room, a lovely black and white building with lots of pointed windows, five steps going up to a heavy pointed door and a low wall along the front with a criss-cross wooden fence on top, which was originally built as a twelve bed hospital and at one time were cottages with three entrance doors and steps at the front.

The Norman church of St Mary's sits just behind the village centre, very large and proud, it marks the hour, quarter, half, three quarter hours and chimes eight a.m. and four p.m. and the bells of St Mary's ring out a different tune every day.

Sunday	'Hanover'	Oh worship the king.
Monday	'A Scottish Air'	Bluebells of Scotland
Tuesday	'An Air for An Irish Melody'	
		My lodging is on the cold ground.
Wednesday	'A Welsh Air'	The Minstrel Boy
Thursday	'An English Air'	The last rose of summer
Friday	'St Thomas for the hymn'	
		Lo He comes with clouds descending
Saturday		Home Sweet Home.

At one time the sexton had to climb into the chamber to wind up the clock but in recent years it has been modified to electric - I bet the sexton is pleased about that.

It has a castle with a moat and a thick stone wall all around, there is a bridge over the moat with two big, heavy, wooden gates, which are always locked. Some parts of the castle has crumbled away. Our mam when we asked why always told us 'It's the little bit that Cromwell knocked about a bit.' We used to laugh and not believe her, but you know something - she was right!

We would climb over the wall when the moat was dry and pick violets and sometimes climb up the other side into the grounds, we found some tunnels but we only ever poked our heads out to look in but would never go more than one or two steps in, it was dark in there and we were too scared.

Tickhill also has a thirteenth century friary which, like the castle is in ruins, all to do with this Oliver Cromwell fellow, but he did a better job on this as there is nothing left but the wall. We were told by other children that there was a tunnel leading from the castle to the friary, but I didn't see how that could be, as it seemed such a long way away from the castle and anyway the Mill Dam was in-between so how could they have tunnelled from the castle to the friary, what did we know!

Now this is where Lindrick begins: just across from the castle gate is the Mill Dam, it has a mill pond which always has ducks swimming around on it, the Mill House has a great wheel and there are two little wooden bridges that you can walk over, they have wooden bars to hold on to, and we would hold on tight as we walked across, or we could walk round the lane in front of the Mill House, something our mam always told us to do, but we liked the wooden bridges, we could see the water under our feet you see, plus from there we could see the water from the dam rushing down a flight of stone steps into the stream which rippled along between the lane and the meadow, what always puzzled me was how did the water calm itself so quickly because, I mean it, it really did splash and bubble when it reached the bottom of the steps: well as I was saying it rippled along and eventually turned to go under the lane, now this is where Lindrick Cottage stands, at a kind of cross-roads, facing Water Lane, with a small holding behind and a little green in front with a large horse chestnut tree - which never failed to produce a glorious mass of pink blossom - standing in the middle, Mam would tell us later that there was always one or the other of us in the pram, under the tree, sleeping or just playing in its shade.

I don't remember the inside of the cottage but it must have been big because there were quite a few of us living there. There was Granddad Marr, that's our mam's dad, our mam and dad, the four of us, Kath, Millie, Margaret, Cyril and Uncle Tom, Millie and Margaret's dad.

Granddad had a Tanworth pig, it was a ginger colour and he would sit us on its back and held us on as it walked around behind the cottage, we weren't frightened, we just used to laugh and when we were lifted off we would run around after it asking for another turn.

I remember playing with my sisters and brother at the beginning of Water Lane, we would play at throwing sticks over the bridge on the side by the meadow and Bower's Walk - you could get to Rowland Bridge if you went along there - then running over to the other side where it came out into Water Lane to see whose stick won, we always argued. We were only ever allowed to play here, if we ventured further down the lane our mam would soon be after us.

Right at the beginning of the lane there were two steps down into the water, they were deep steps and we had to hold onto the bank and stretch our legs to reach the next step, not our Lionel though, he had long legs and it was easy for him. The steps were very handy for catching our sticks when we played. Once Lionel said he would sail down the stream, so he got some cardboard and went down the steps, - funny we thought he would be able to after all the water did run pretty quickly. He held the cardboard on the water, sat on it and sank, we screamed, Mam came from nowhere and got him out and we had to stay in for the rest of the day.

There was a big house across the lane to the left of the cottage with big wooden gates at the side. Miss Clarke lived there all on her own I would have been too frightened to do that. We didn't see her very much, but at Easter time she would take us into her great big kitchen to show us her little yellow chicks that were hatching by the fire, oh they were so lovely, all fluffy and toppling over on their little legs, and she would give us an Easter egg, not one with a little chick in, this one was chocolate, and she always gave us a Christmas present. She was nice and I wished that she had someone to stay with her and keep her company sometimes.

Across the lane in front of the cottage was a big, white house with a long drive going up to the front which was high up on a sort of bank, and that made is look even bigger, well our Millie was in service there, that means that she would make the beds and clean things for the lady, it was all very posh, we never ever went into the house.

Our dad's name was Thomas Cooper and he had a brother, Henry Cooper - funny that isn't it? Although at the time, as far as we knew they were the only Thomas and Henry Cooper in the whole world. Our mam's name was Rose Ann Marr and she had a sister Annie, our mam married Thomas Cooper and her sister Annie married Henry Cooper. She also had a brother Jim, and another sister Carrie, we never knew our Aunt Carrie, you see she died and left two young girls Millicent and Margaret and an older boy, Frank who was in the army. Millie and Margaret came to live with our mam and dad when they were only seven and eight years old because they didn't have a mam any more, but they did have a dad who was our Uncle Tom and he came to live with us as well.

We all loved our mam. She was tall with brown hair, which she wore in a bun. She didn't make herself fancy or anything and she didn't have any posh clothes, she said she had no need of them. She was good and kind to everyone and always helped people in any way she could, even though we didn't have much money. She never thought of herself, always making sure that we had all we needed and that everyone was happy. She was our mam, but to everyone else, family or friends, she was Aunt Rose.

She was the very heart of our family that everyone turned to, she usually had her pinnie on and be up to her elbows in flour while baking, cooking something over the fire or in the oven. Washing everything by hand, scrubbing dirty things up and down her wash board, and there was a lot of us to wash for I can tell you, she had two very heavy flat irons which had to be put on the

Yorkshire range to get hot, then she would lift one off and place it in a shiny, smooth holder, then she could start to iron the clothes, changing the irons as they grew cold. Our mam could do anything. She was good at shielding us from anything she thought would upset us, saying 'What they don't know won't hurt them.' And so unbeknown to us at this time, Mam had fallen and hurt her leg on a piece of wood and it was hurting her quite a bit. She hardly ever went out, she was too busy doing things, if anyone asked her to go anywhere with them, she would say 'You go, I'll stay here and get on.' She was always 'Getting on' with something.

CHAPTER TWO

SUNDERLAND STREET

We all moved from Lindrick Cottage, that is: Mam, Dad, Grandad, Uncle Tom, Cyril, Kath, Millie, Margaret and the four of us, to 'The Gas House' why was it called that? I think that it had gas works on the ground behind at some time before we moved there, it stood on its own on the edge of the village at the bottom of Sunderland Street and at one time must have been a garage as it had a pit that you could drive a car over to work underneath, except we didn't have a car so it wasn't much good to us. It was a nice house with a large living room at the back with a Yorkshire range, there was a large cellar with stone steps down and lots of stone shelves to keep the food cold and a meat safe, this was really just a wooden box on short legs with a wire mesh door and would keep meat nice and fresh. Our mam used to keep the milk down there an all. We used to get the milk from Rawson's Farm which was half way down Sunderland Street next to Stocks Meadow, we would leave a milk can on our way to school and pick it up on the way home, we liked doing this as we had to go into the milking parlour to get the can and if they were still milking the cows the farm-hand would squirt the milk at us trying to get us wet and make us squeal, and the other thing that we would do if we had to wait was ... now don't you tell our mam ... we would pinch cow cake and locus beans, in other words 'the cow's fodder' Doreen really liked the beans, she's funny! So while she munched them we would watch the milk running down what looked to me like our mam's washing board, until our milk was ready, anyway as I was saying apart from the cellar where the milk went the house had two rooms at the front and four bedrooms upstairs. There was no electricity or gas for that matter, but Mam had some big glass paraffin lamps that would light up the whole room, and we had candles to light us to bed. The dry toilet was at the bottom of the garden, a long walk all the way down the long garden path and every night we had to do a wee before we went to bed, if it was dark outside Mam would send us off with a candle to light our way and although we held our hand around the flame, sometimes the candle went out and that would have us scurrying back to the house like the devil was on our heels. There was quite a large area of ground at the back and side of the house and a shallow ditch running along the bottom, all the way around the side and under Sunderland Street where it appeared again in Mr and Mrs Glasbey's garden, they lived in the tiniest little cottage which at one time was the old Toll House and was used when cattle were driven through Tickhill to Bawtry's River Idle and it sits on the corner of Common Lane and Sunderland Street, the garden runs along Sunderland Street behind a low, stone wall - sometimes when we were waiting for a bus to Harworth we sat on the wall then we could see the whole garden and wave to Mr and Mrs Glasbey, now just before it went under the road there were four steps down (more steps down to water) we couldn't believe our luck. These steps were covered in tar and when it was hot and sunny the tar would melt, and we would pop the tar bubbles with our fingers and get tar all over our hands, we played on these steps a lot. There were two pipes going across the ditch near our tar steps, one was thin and the other quite fat, we sometimes walked across the fat one if we dared, if not we would sit with one leg either side and shuffle across, you should have seen the state of our knickers after we had been doing that. One day Doreen's friend Alice was playing with us, she had a white dress on and tried to walk along the pipe and fell into the muddy water, our Doreen didn't go back to her house to play that day. When it hadn't rained for a while and everything was dry we would bob our heads down and walk under the road to Mr and Mrs Glasbey's tiny little cottage and come up in their garden, they had an apple tree and we would pinch apples, it wasn't as if we had to as she would have given us some if we had asked, I'm sure she must have been watching us but pretending she didn't know. She had a pretty garden with lots of flowers, a winding path and a rose arch, unlike ours, which was more like a big yard except that we did have a lilac tree by the side gate and a rose arch across our long path, but I think hers was prettier than ours, it was only our Doreen, Enid and me that went into the garden, our Lionel used to be busy playing with his friend Walter.

Mrs Glasbey never seemed to mind us popping up and she would let us wear her high-heeled shoes to walk up and down the path, we would go into her little cottage and help her bake cakes and pies sometimes, and one day she gave Doreen a book of poems which Doreen loved and she would often read some of them to me and our Enid, her favourite one was 'Queen of the May' and 'Mary Call the Cattle Home' was another. Once Mrs Glasbey took us with her for a few days to Cockhill Farm which was not very far away from Tickhill and we played on the haystacks and had lots of fun, I remember watching her make butter, then with two big, flat wooden spoon things and she would pat the butter, weigh it and if it was too heavy she would take some off until she got it right, then pat it into a nice square and put it into some special kind of paper to keep it fresh. We liked it there and we liked Mrs Glasbey as well.

Mrs Brown was Mam's best friend and she always called once a week for a chat. It was a long way for her to come as she lived in Westgate. We never heard what they chatted about as Mam would say 'Now go and play while I make Mrs Brown a cup of tea.' In other words - children should be seen and not heard. Sometimes she would call in the evening and Mam would cook tripe and onions for the two of them. Mrs Brown had been Mam's friend for a long time and her daughter Mary was our Kath, Millie and Margaret's friend.

We used to play mothers and fathers, dressing up and pretending to get married, and our garden path was the aisle except this isle only had our dry toilet at the end - phew, what a thought. Once when it was Doreen's turn to be the bride, we put a washer on her finger but when she tried to take it off it was stuck and we were all in trouble because our dad had to take her to the blacksmiths on the cross bar of his bike to get it cut off, I expect she was very frightened, bet she cried an all, anyway I'm glad it wasn't me, I would have cried a lot louder than our Doreen.

Our mam sometimes bought fish for dinner, and when she had cut the heads off and thrown them away, we used to get them out of the bin and bury them in little graves that we would dig in rows by the garden path, then we would go into the field next to our house and pick daisies and kingcups, and put these in any little jars that we could find in the dustbin and then say a prayer for them, sometimes Mam didn't see them for days, but when she did she would make us dig them up and put them back in the bin, but it didn't stop us doing it the next time she cooked fish.

Our Lionel's friend, Walter lived further still outside Tickhill village than we did, he had to go along Spital, which is the continuation of Sunderland Street, it has trees that started just by our house all the way down on both sides of the road and in the summer when the leaves were on the trees, they almost touched to make a long arch right down to the bottom and in the winter when the frost and snow came it looked so pretty, just like Fairyland. Half way down, is Black Lane there is a red brick house with steps going up to the front door which seemed really high up, we never played down Black Lane, maybe it was the name that put us off, just along from there is a bridge where the water which drains off the fields runs under the road and eventually reaches our tar steps, a little further down are one or two large houses but you can only catch a glimpse of them in the autumn or winter when the leaves have fallen, there's a pretty cross-roads at the bottom, with a very large house named 'Sandrock' on the corner of Spital Hill which like the others is out of sight in the summer, there is a large area of grass going around into Rossington Road with a tree growing out of what looks like a giant plant pot made of grey stone. We always stopped and scrambled up to sit on the grass under the tree, across the road from Sandrock is a copse, we called it Bluebell Wood, it was like a lovely blue carpet when the bluebells were out, too pretty to play on - now Walter had to go straight across and up Spital Hill on the Bawtry Road to where he lived. He used to play a lot with our Lionel.

Once they made a cart out of some old pram wheels they had found, they put wooden boards on and two long pieces of wood for handles and some rope for reins, then, Walter would be the horse and Lionel the farmer and they would give each other rides up and down the long path that led to our toilet, changing jobs, farmer for horse when the horse got tired. They used to let us have a ride, but we didn't like it much, it was very bumpy and hurt our bums, but not only that, they would expect us to take a turn at being the horse, we used to have a ride then run away to play on our own, usually on the tar steps. Our mam would always know when we had been on the tar steps because we would have tar on our shoes and sometimes on our knickers an all where we had sat on the steps, we always had it on our hands because we couldn't resist popping the tar bubbles when it was hot, we just loved playing with them.

One day when Walter came to play, we joined in playing ball, throwing it and kicking it about, well we must have got over enthusiastic and the ball ended up in a sort of loft, anyway, Lionel and Walter found a long ladder and put it up against the wall beneath the loft. Walter said he would go up, so he set off climbing the ladder and laughing as he went, when he got to the top he looked down at us and said, 'Don't forget the diver sir' I think it was a kind of saying grown-ups used. Anyway off he went to find the ball, we kept calling 'Have you found it?' and he would shout 'No, not yet.' After a while he didn't answer our calls so Lionel, thinking that he was mucking about, went up the ladder to look for him while we waited at the bottom, getting very frightened. Lionel said he couldn't find him and came down. We didn't know where to look for him and decided to go and tell our mam that he was lost, but when we got in the door, there was Walter laying down crying and saying 'Don't let me die.' You see he had fallen through the floor in the loft, down to where the pit thing was and he was hurt and wouldn't stop crying. Our mam told us it was a good job that a workman cycling by saw him laying there and brought him in, I thought it was a good job an all, otherwise we would have thought he'd gone home and not got lost after all, and we would have forgotten about looking for him.

Now our Millie had a lovely cream pram, it was big and bouncy, she didn't have a baby to put in it yet, so she put Walter in and with our Kath's help pushed him all the way home, even up Spital Hill and that's blinking steep. When they got back they said that Walter was saying, 'Don't let me die,' all the way home but, he was going to be all right. We had to stay in for the rest of the day and Walter wasn't allowed to play with our Lionel for a long time afterwards.

Mr and Mrs Crossland lived in Sunderland Street in a cottage near Vine Terrace, and Mam would send one or the other of us to pop in and make sure they were alright 'cos they were a bit old, about like our granddad I suppose. Grandad lived with us and he slept in one of the rooms at the front of the house, downstairs, he had a great big bed in there 'cos he was a very big man and he had a lovely white moustache and he would sit for most of the day in his big wooden armchair and twiddle both sides of his moustache so they were always sticking up in a little curl on each cheek, like 'chapel hat pegs' our mam would say, she said that when our hair was sticking up as well. Our mam used to make us laugh and sometimes when we did something silly she would laugh and get the giggles till she had to sit down, we liked it when we made her laugh.

CHAPTER THREE

THE GYPSIES

Common Lane started along the side of Mr and Mrs Glasbey's cottage. Every year the gypsies would come to stay a little way down the lane, we never seemed to see them come or go they just appeared and when they had stayed for a few weeks they would disappear. Sometimes there would be three or four caravans. They had lots of horses which were kept on long ropes, staked on the grass verge that had lots of grass for them to eat, they also had dogs that seemed to bark a lot and they tied them up to the wheels of the caravans and put bowls of water and food for them.

Their caravans were painted in lots of colours, blues, yellows and greens in pretty patterns and windows with curtains held back each side so that you could see the flowers and ornaments inside. Wooden steps led up to the door which was in two halves just like Mr Rawson had in his farmyard so that the horse could look out if it wanted to. Sometimes we could see inside if they had both halves open but we didn't get too near in case they ran away with us.

Every year when they came, one of the gypsy ladies would call at our house to ask our mam if she would bake the pies she had made in her oven, Mam always did, and as we had a Yorkshire range that was always hot she never minded, Mam would always make the gypsy lady a cup of tea, but the gypsy lady would never go into our house, she would just sit on the doorstep and drink it while she chatted to our mam. The gypsy lady had a little girl about our age and she would stay and play with us sometimes. When we had been playing all day and came in tired and dirty, Mam would get a bowl of warm water to wash our hands and face, she would be mumbling to herself as she washed each one of us saying 'Look at the colour of your neck, I'm sure I don't know if you are one of my kiddies or if you belong to the gypsies down the lane, mind you, their little kiddie is probably cleaner than you lot.' We got called 'you lot' a lot when we were all together like 'Come on you lot time for bed,' or 'Where have you lot been till now.' It was quicker than saying all our names, you see.

When the pies were cooked and had cooled down, Mam would give them to us to take down the lane to the gypsy, we never liked doing this very much as the horses and dogs frightened us and we didn't like getting too near to them and all the way there we would be telling each other not to go inside the caravan although it was tempting because it did look very pretty when we peeped in sometimes and also not to eat any pie should we be offered any, just in case it had poison in the bit they tried to give us. What a thing to think!

I remember the day our Kath and Millie were going up to the village and I was with them, holding on to our Kath's hand, looking up at her I just thought she looked a bit poorly, her face was very thin and she was tired, and I asked her if I should call her Auntie Kath, maybe I thought it would cheer her up a bit. She just smiled down at me and said 'No, because I'm your sister.' Well I didn't' know that, I suppose everyone just thought I did, but I didn't, not only that, but, I suppose she thought she had better make sure that I knew that Cyril, was my brother, and it's a good job she did because I didn't know that either, you see Cyril was away a lot, I think he was doing his National Service as I remember him in his army uniform, anyway he was older than our Kath and they were both much older than the four of us, and it was all something to do with our dad having to go away from home to find work, so when he came back to work nearer home, that's when they had us.

Uncle Tom hadn't been living with us very long when we got the heart-breaking news that he had been killed in a car accident on the Bawtry Road, so now Millie and Margaret didn't have a mam or dad, but they would be alright because they were going to share ours, I suppose they must have been sad and would have liked to have their own but our mam and dad will make them happy again, I just know they will. We will miss our Uncle Tom and all 'cos he used to go to Doncaster every Saturday and when he came home he always had a big bag of sweets for us, which he gave to our mam and she would give us two or three every day, they were always the same, fruity, in the shape of a fish and covered with sugar, they were big enough to hold by the tail and suck all the sugar off the head, umm, they were lovely and lasted a long time if you just sucked them, which we always did, as Mam said if we crunched them our teeth would go bad and fall out.

CHAPTER FOUR

WAR

It was while we were here that the war started. We were not told, I suppose we were too young and 'Children were seen and not heard.' Mam used to say that, she also used to say 'What they don't know won't hurt them.'

We had to have black curtains at all the windows so that the lights didn't shine outside, but we only had oil lamps and candles so there wasn't that much light to hide, but Mam wouldn't let us peep through the black-out curtains, so that put a stop to our spying on Kath, Millie and Margaret when they came home late for the time being anyway.

We now had a gas mask each and had to carry it everywhere we went, it seemed funny, the gas masks when our house was called The Gas House, they were in a square cardboard box with a long string handle that you could put over your head and put one arm through as well, so that you had your hands free to put them in your pockets if it was cold or to hold each others hands, everyone had their names on the cardboard boxes. We took them to school every day and sometimes we would have a 'gas mask drill' this would mean taking them out of the box so that the teacher could help us to put them on, yuk! They were horrid things, all made of rubber stuff with wide rubber criss-cross straps that went over your head, they always got tangled up and we could never get them right, that's why the teacher had to help, these straps used to pull your hair when you put them on and took them off and I hated my hair being pulled. The mask that went over your face was rubber and very tight, it had a kind of window made of plastic so you could see where you were going and at the bottom there was this round, heavy grill so you could breath and talk through it, it made you sound funny and look really funny an all, because it made you look like a pig with a big snout, if you sucked your cheeks in, the snout bit would move. The whole school soon learned how to do this and we used to giggle at each other through the window bit and sometimes we would laugh so much that the window would steam up, we never kept them on for very long and we never seemed to be able to get them back into the box properly either. Oh I did hope we would never have to wear them for a whole day.

Most nights when we had the black-out curtains up, the planes would come over the house, lots and lots at a time, they were big and came over very low, our dad said they were going to bomb Sheffield, and he used to go out of the back door to take a look at them. Once when we asked if we could see them, Mam said 'No and anyway you only have your nighties on.' Not our Lionel though he wore pyjamas, plus she said 'It is too dangerous.' But Dad said it would be alright so Mam let us out of the door and told us to stay behind Dad, when we looked up we saw lots of big, dark aeroplanes droning across the sky on their way to bomb Sheffield, but strangely enough it hadn't frightened us.

What did frighten us was, the day we came out of school and turned into Sunderland Street to find lots of soldiers with guns, crawling on their bellies along the side of the road all the way down. We were so frightened that we ran all the way home crying, and another time when me and our Enid were playing in the garden with our dolls just beside the hedge that ran between us and the field behind, when the hedge started to move and a soldier with a gun and a helmet with leaves and things tucked in it, poked his head through and made us jump so much we were shaking and crying, running in to tell our mam, well she went out into the field and gave him a good telling off for scaring us, but he wasn't the only soldier in the field, there were lots of them all crawling around, they were training or something like the ones we had seen in Sunderland Street, but the soldier didn't do it on purpose, he didn't know we were there, we must have been playing quietly for once. We saw convoys quite a few times, we would spot them coming along Harworth Road, lots and lots of trucks close behind each other and we would wait at the front of our house and wave to them as they went by, there were lots of soldiers billeted in Tickhill, in two or three of the big houses up by the Butter Cross.

A little way up Sunderland Street was a farm and the farm gate was set back on a very wide grass verge, and usually at about the time that we were coming home from school there would be some farm workers having a drink and a cigarette and our mam said they were Italian prisoners of war, and we were not to stop and talk to them, her words were always 'Don't stop and talk to the Ities.' We never did, we always hurried by but they did wave and smile and speak in a funny way that we didn't understand, I would like to think they were saying hello to us and that we reminded them of the children they have left behind.

It was about this time that Mollie came to stay with us bringing her son Barry and little daughter Gloria with her, she was even smaller than our Enid. Mam told us they were evacuees from Coventry and had to stay with us as the big, dark aeroplanes were bombing Coventry and their house wasn't safe for them to live in, not like ours was. Maybe the aeroplanes that came over our house went there after they had been to Sheffield. Mollie's husband, Sid didn't stay with us, you see he was in the army, but he did come to stay sometimes, only for short visits though, anyway the good thing was that now we had a little girl in the house who was smaller than any of us so we would be able to look after her, and maybe be in charge for a time. There was always someone or other in charge of us, even our Doreen was in charge of me and our Enid sometimes but we had never been in charge of anyone, maybe we could be in charge of Gloria, oh! We would feel right grown-up if we did that, but if not, then Gloria could be our little playmate.

Mam gave Mollie the big room downstairs, across the hall from Grandad's at the front of the house she had a big bed to sleep in with Gloria, and when Sid came sometimes, he would sleep in it too. We liked Mollie, she was tall and slim with black curly hair, and she didn't talk like us, she talked funny, Gloria's hair was lighter with really tight, tiny curls all over her head.

They hadn't been with us very long when one morning as we past by Mollie's bedroom door on our way to the living room for breakfast we heard a cry and when we asked our mam what it was she said 'That's our Mickey.' You see Mollie was pregnant when she arrived and he was her new little son - the name stuck and from that day he was known as our Mickey, well we wanted to see him right away so we finished our breakfast as fast as we could then Mam took us to see him - the first new-born baby that we had ever seen, his hair was just like Gloria's, a mass of tiny curls like little springs, we would pull the curls straight, not hard though, then let them go, to see them spring tight again, we didn't pull their hair hard, nobody likes their hair pulled, me most of all.

Gloria came to Sunday school - with us in charge of her - she must have found it a very long way to walk because she was a lot smaller than us, in fact too small to go to infant school, but she was soon coming everywhere with us to play. Once we took her down Common Lane for a little walk and she went into the hedgerow. Before long she was crying for us to get her out, and when we got to her she was all tangled up in a bush, and she had sticky buds on her clothes which we started to pull off before taking her home, then we saw her hair, yuk! It had loads of sticky buds in her curls and when we tried to pull them out she started screaming, she obviously didn't like her hair being pulled either, so we had to take her home for her mam to do it, we didn't' hang around to watch nor did we mention sticky buds again.

CHAPTER FIVE

BATH NIGHT

Saturday night was bath night. Mam had a tin bath which used to hang on a nail outside, next to the big barrel that caught the rain water, Mam always used this water for our hair, she said it would keep it soft and shiny, anyway she would get the bath down and bring it into the living room, the one that had the Yorkshire range in and put it on the big square wooden table. The Yorkshire range always had a fire going and the kettles were always full of hot water just sitting on the top waiting to be used, it also had a water tank at one side and that was always full of hot water which could be ladled out into the bowl in the sink to wash dishes and things and also to fill our bath. Sometimes if our mam had been busy and needed a sit down, Kath, Millie and Margaret would bath us; anyway there was usually one to wash, one to dry and one to dress us. We always argued whose turn it was to go first, you see the bath couldn't be emptied after each one, sometimes if one of us was really dirty, then even if it was our turn to go first we would have to go last, I hated it when that happened because the next Saturday we would argue all over again whose turn it was.

The other thing that wasn't very nice was the senopods we had to drink, our mam used to make this medicine, she would get these pod things, put them in a big jug and pour water in, then leave them in the cellar all week, we dreaded that jug coming out, that stuff tasted awful, kept our bowels open Mam said. The other thing we would have to take if we had, just a bit of a cold was brimstone and treacle and if we had a chesty cough Mam would rub goose grease on our chest and back, and we would have to sleep in our liberty bodice, not our Lionel though he had to keep his vest on. So what with the cod liver oil and malt that we had to take every day at school, the senopods, brimstone and treacle and goose grease. I suppose we could be seen as clean and healthy kiddies. After our bath and hair wash, we would be all warm and cosy in our wincyette night-gowns, not our Lionel though, he had pyjamas then Kath, Millie and Margaret would rag our hair so that our hair would have ringlets in on Sunday when we went to chapel. The rags were very uncomfortable to sleep in but we didn't mind because on Sunday it would look lovely. After all that we would have a warm drink, sometimes warm milk with bread in it, that was called pobs, then it would be up to bed, we had candles but we were not allowed to hold them indoors even though they were in a candlestick holder, these were enamel and looked like a saucer with a handle on and a bit sticking up in the middle for the candle to stand up in, we had quite a few of these. We slept three in a bed, that's me, Doreen and Enid, Lionel had a small bed all to himself in the same room. Our Doreen used to sleep walk sometimes so Mam told me to put my arm around her to stop her getting out of bed, but if she did get out, not to wake her, just come straight down to let Mam know, but whenever I put my arm around Doreen she would push it away telling me to 'Ger off' so she got away every time, I would ask her where she was going, sometimes she was going to play with her friend Alice or going down to get her doll some clean clothes, and sometimes for more dinner, then I would rush past her and go down stairs to tell our mam so she could deal with her when she reached the living room. Kath, Millie and Margaret used to take us up the stairs and tuck us in. They would tell us to go straight to sleep or we would have Mam after us, but we never did, we would soon find something to giggle about and before we knew it we would be getting louder and jumping around on the bed and Mam would shout up to us to be quiet, she didn't come up if she could get us to be quiet by calling, I think her leg was hurting her a lot these days but she never complained, then later on, as our bedroom was at the front of the house we would peep through the curtains to see Kath, Millie and Margaret coming home from a dance or the pictures, sometimes with their young men and sometimes they kissed, well that would start us giggling again and we would put our hands over our mouths so no one would know we had seen them. Kathleen's young man was Burt, and Millie's young man was Arthur, both serving in the air force and based at Finningley, which was close to Rossington where Dad worked. Margaret's young man, Ernest was a local boy, his family lived in Rowland Cottage, by the Mill Dam and Margaret was able to see more of her young man, she could also spend some time at his home and have tea with his mam. Kath and Millie on the other hand could only see their young men when they had a pass to leave the base, which they seemed to be able to do quite a bit and we peeped through the curtains quite a bit an all.

You know something, we were very lucky because we had four mam's looking after us, Mam, Kath, Millie and

Margaret, they were all there for us, making sure we came to no harm, kissing us better when we were hurt, tucking us into bed, making us feel safe and sound and smacking our bums when we were naughty, but oh we were loved.

Apart from helping to bath us Kath, Millie and Margaret, would always be busy knitting things for us, in the winter they would knit warm pixie hats which really kept our ears warm, with mittens and scarves to match, they made jumpers and cardigans with pretty patterns on the front, and Dutch bonnets, which they made from felt material in lovely colours and they embroidered flowers on each side, they were nice and we wore them for Sunday school when it was cold. Not our Lionel though he had gloves, scarves and v-necked jumpers. Once they knitted identical dresses in a maroon colour for us, they had a collar with four buttons down the front, almost to the waist and the skirt was flared, when we tried them on, I said I didn't like mine because it was too long so they put elastic in the waist so I could hitch it up to make it shorter. The things they did for a quiet life, they had the patience of a saint.

CHAPTER SIX

SUNDAY SCHOOL

Every Sunday we would go to Sunday school in the morning and again in the afternoon. We had to walk even further than we did to our infant school, we went up to the Butter Cross and into Northgate, then walked a little way past the parish room, crossed the road and there we were at the Wesleyan Chapel. We were too little to go into the big chapel where the organ was so we went along the side, past some tiny cottages and into a small room at the back of the chapel, quite a lot of children came here on a Sunday, we had little chairs to sit on, like the ones in our infant school. We would say our prayers and sing songs, like 'Jesus Wants Me For A Sunbeam' then the teacher would tell us a story from the bible, we would sing some more and then it was time for home.

Just across the road from the chapel was the working men's club and Dad used to go there every Sunday for a pint, when we came out of chapel, we would go over to him and he would bring out lemonade and crisps, when we had finished Dad walked home with us. Mam would have the Sunday roast cooking, then one or the other of us would go to the shop near Vine Terrace to get some shandy in a big jug for Grandad. Sometimes he let us have a taste, but we didn't like it, but we always tasted it the following Sunday, just in case we liked it a bit better than before, but we never did.

Whitsuntide was the best of all because we would have a new dress, shoes and a pretty straw bonnet, not our Lionel though, he had new trousers, boots and cap. On Whit Sunday we would go into the big chapel where there would be a rostrum, made especially for us, it had steps going all the way up and we would stand on the steps so that everyone could see us, even the people in the pews that were up the stairs could see us. Mr Mason would sit at the organ and play so that we could sing our little heads off for them all. We would all have a special poem or verse that we had learned off by heart, to say all on our own, that was a bit scary, and my knees would be knocking. After that came prize-giving and then we went home to proudly show Mam our prize. Another special Sunday was Easter, when we would rush home to look for the Easter eggs that Mam always made for us.

Once a year we went on the chapel trip to the seaside, we had to put our names down, then we would take some money every Sunday and the teacher would write the amount in a book, especially for the seaside. When the day came we were all so excited, Mam packed sandwiches and cakes and bottles of pop and Dad gave us spending money, either Kath, Millie or Margaret would take us, our mam always wanted two of them with us, Mam would come sometimes, but mostly she stayed at home to 'Get on with things', she never worried because she knew we were in good hands. The big coach, sometimes even two would be at the Butter Cross and we would scramble on as fast as we could, wanting to eat our food and drink the pop before we even sat down. When we got to the seaside, usually Skegness, Cleethorpes or Mablethorpe our Kath liked Mablethorpe the best of all, the first thing we did was to buy a paper hat, we kept them on all day, even when we went on a roundabout and the donkeys, we bought candyfloss and got our hands sticky then we would laugh with each other saying we were 'stuck up', we always bought a stick of rock to take home with us. On the coach home we would still be wearing the hats, and only when our mam has seen us in them would we take them off. We were four, tired, grubby kiddies that just wanted to go to bed.

I remember one Sunday, we came out of Sunday school looking very nice in our Sunday best. It was raining a bit as we crossed the road to see Dad, well he had the dog, a spaniel with him, we hadn't had him very long, in fact we hadn't even given him a name yet but he was pleased to see us and wanted to jump up. Dad stopped him. We had our lemonade and crisps then we got on our way home, we asked our dad if we could take a turn at holding the lead, he didn't want us to do that because we had our best clothes on. We kept on and on until he said we could, as soon as he said that we were all fighting to be the first, and in the end we all had hold of him and he got so excited that he began to run and jump about and then instead of letting his lead go we hung on and ended up being pulled along the wet grass verge. Dad was horrified, he caught hold of the dog and tried to clean us up a bit before taking us home.

When we got home Mam went mad and blamed Dad for letting us hold him in the first place. We stayed back and let Dad take all the blame. Mam told him to take the dog back to the man he had bought it from, Dad tried to talk her round but she was having none of it and insisted the dog would have to go. The next time Dad went to work he took the dog with him, putting a long piece of rope on his collar, he got on his bike and set off down Spital, you see, Dad had got the dog from a man who worked with him and he lived in Rossington where the pit was. Dad came back without the dog. We were upset as we liked him even if we couldn't take him for walks. But the next morning the dog was sitting by the back door waiting for something to eat and Dad had to get on his bike and take him back again, we never saw him after that.

CHAPTER SEVEN

OUR DAD

Our dad wasn't very tall, well anyway he was shorter than Mam. He worked very hard and we didn't see very much of him when we were really little as we went to bed early. He was a nice dad and would never smack us. If we had been naughty, Mam would say, 'I'll tell your father when he comes home.' But we knew he wouldn't do anything, he might say 'now try and behave yourselves you little buggers.' If he was home and we were naughty, Mam would say 'Father, can you sort this lot out.' And Dad would either say 'That's your department mother.' Or he would just make to take his belt off as though to smack us and we would run out squealing, 'Oh, no Dad don't.' He never did and what's more we knew he wouldn't. Our mam always called him 'Father' when she was talking to us, but when she was calling him for something or talking to grown-ups about him then she would call him Cooper, I suppose she did call him Tom when they were discussing something, but we never heard them discuss anything, you know, the seen but not heard thing.

When Dad was home he would just wear trousers and shirt and most times a waistcoat as well, but his jacket was never far away as he would always put it on if there was a knock at the door before he answered it, you see he would know that it must be a stranger because the door was never locked and anyone else would just walk in calling hello on the way.

When he went out on a Sunday for his pint, he would always wear a suit with a waistcoat and he had a pocket watch and chain and he kept the watch in one waistcoat pocket then the chain would go over the buttons to the other side and it had a coin hanging on the chain. I liked our dad wearing that, oh! And he wore a flat cap an all.

He always cut our hair and we all looked the same, we had a fringe and the rest was cut all the way round, just below our ears, not our Lionel though, he had a short back and sides, that's what our dad used to call it, we all had brown hair which was very, very straight. Dad mended our shoes and everybody else's as well, he got the leather from Mr Timpson who had a shoe shop in the village and also mended shoes, but he didn't mind selling leather to our dad.

Dad had a bike, everyone seemed to have a bike, hardly anyone had a car. He worked at a pit in Rossington, which was down Spital turn left at the cross-road into Rossington Road. There was another pit in Harworth, which was also down Spital and right at the cross-roads, all of a sudden we knew where there were three pits, except that we had only seen the one at our house - you know, the one that Walter nearly fell into. We were soon to learn how very different they were.

Our dad had always gone to the pit before we had woken up in the morning, but Mam would tell us when he was coming home so we could look out for him, we would stand on the grass verge we were not allowed on the road. We used to poke our heads out, stretching our necks to see who could spot him first, as soon as he was in sight we would run as fast as we could to him and he would get off his bike and wait for us to reach him, then he would open his 'snap tin' this was sort of metal in the shape of a very, very thick slice of bread and the top lid went all the way over the bottom, it had a handle that could swing, Dad said when he was at work he could hang it on his belt, he always wore a belt. Anyway as I was saying, he opened it saying he didn't think he had saved us anything because he had been so hungry, but he was only kidding, and we always got some home-made cake or a bit of sandwich, I'm sure Mam used to put extra in for us then with Dad back on his bike and us squealing and giggling around him, he lifted first one then the other of us onto the cross bar for a little ride as we headed for home.

On Saturdays Dad used to work at the cinema in Harworth, he was the doorman and he had a uniform with brass buttons on. He cycled there, and since Dad worked at the cinema Mam used to let us go to the Saturday matinee, she would take us over the road to wait for the bus and make sure we were on safely. There were usually some of our friends on the bus already, as they would have got on at the Butter Cross. The bus stopped just outside the cinema where Dad would be waiting for us if he wasn't busy, if he wasn't there then we just went to the lady that sold the tickets and she would send us in, we usually took one or two friends with us and we gave them our pixie hats to put on so she would think they were one of us, she must have thought our dad had an awful lot of kiddies. At the matinee the children could only sit in the first six rows that was so

Dad could keep his eye on everyone. If there was a 'rowdy bunch' that's what Dad called them he would sit us at the back out of the way but we would rather have been down at the front with them all, at the end Dad always took us across the road to wait for the bus home, he would put us on then go back to lock everything up before he cycled home. Mam didn't have to worry about us getting off the bus as it stopped right outside our house and we would jump off and run through the gate and in the house to see Mam. When Dad got home he always made us laugh by asking us if we had grit in our eyes after seeing Roy Rogers and Trigger kicking up the dust.

Our mam told us when we were a little older, that before we were born our dad was in the First World War, and his leg got hurt badly. He had to come home until it was better and she went to meet him at Doncaster train station. When the train arrived there were lots and lots of soldiers getting off - they were all wounded - some so badly they needed carrying, she was looking everywhere for him but he found her. Mam said that she didn't recognise him, he looked so thin and ill, and if he hadn't seen her she may have walked right by and gone home. When his leg was mended, he had to go back to the war. Mam said he was so frightened and didn't want to go back as he had seen so many terrible things. The trenches where they had to fight and sleep were cold and wet and soldiers got blown up every day. He went back because if he hadn't he would have been shot at dawn and Mam says that was the truth of it. Uncle Harry was in that war too.

Uncle Harry looked a lot like our dad, he wasn't very tall and he wore a flat cap like our dad did - Uncle Harry walked with a limp and that was something to do with the war as well, he used to make us laugh when ever we saw him and we all loved to see him.

One day Uncle Harry called to see Mam and Dad because, Auntie Annie was feeling a little bit down - you see she couldn't' have children of her own and Uncle Harry came to ask if he could borrow one of the girls, just for a little while to make her happy. Well our mam had little girls coming out of her ears, so she said 'Which one would you like?' Uncle Harry pointed to me and said 'I'll give you tuppence for that one.'- Mam said 'Goo on then' and off we went. They lived near the Mill Dam just a little bit further on from Mrs Brown. From that day on Uncle Harry always called me Tuppney. One day Mam sent a message to Auntie Annie saying that she had a pair of boots for me for school and could Uncle Harry call and get them. Well when I heard about them I started showing off saying that I didn't want to go to school in boots - the only boots that I had seen were the black lace ups that our Lionel wore, and I wasn't going anywhere in boy's boots whether my feet were cold or not and besides that everyone would laugh at me. Uncle Harry picked them up from home and gave them to me saying 'Now just you have a look and you had better like them or your mam will be after me.' So I looked and found they were nice ones with fur inside, only for girls - I was glad Mam hadn't sent them back to the shop, otherwise I would have been very sorry when I saw Doreen and Enid wearing theirs.

CHAPTER EIGHT
INFANT SCHOOL

We had quite a long way to walk to our infant school, which was all the way up Sunderland Street almost to the Butter Cross, it was at the end of Tithes Lane, just a short lane between Jarvis shop and the high stone wall of the vicarage garden. It was a very small school, a schoolhouse rather than a proper school.

Every morning Mam would get us ready, making sure we were tidy, then looking at us would say 'You'll do', our mam always said that, never saying we looked lovely - that would make us vain - she said. She would always give us two sweets, 'Not to be eaten in class' so sometimes we would keep them in our knicker pocket with our clean hanky, we were also given a spoon and of course our gas masks over our shoulder. She would see us across the road, telling us to stay together and behave ourselves, and reminded us to bring our spoons home.

We always arrived at school in time to have a little play before the teacher came out and blew her whistle. When she did we got in our line in the playground with our spoons at the ready, and one by one she would give us, a spoonful of cod liver oil and straight after we would get malt, which was brown and sticky, but much nicer than the cod liver oil, that made us feel sick. There was nowhere to wash our spoons so we just licked them clean and put them in our pocket, not the one we had our sweets in, but another one, not our Lionel though he put his in his coat pocket where his sweets would be all sticky and tangled up in string, he always had string in his pocket. At morning playtime we would have a little bottle of milk and a straw, the milk was always left outside in the playground and was either too warm in the summer or freezing cold in the winter, sometimes with ice on the top.

The thing I remember most of all was the pot-bellied stove that stood in the classroom with a high fireguard going all the way around it, and in the winter it would have coke inside and it would get very hot, and made the classroom lovely and warm. In the winter months Mollie would bring us something hot for our lunch, you see it was too far for us to go home and Mollie had a bike with a basket on the front so she could bring us, maybe jacket potatoes with butter, or home-made soup with bread that Mam made, and we would sit around the pot-bellied stove on our little chairs, Mollie sat on one as well as there were no big chairs, just the piano stool, and heaven forbid if she sat on that, that was the pride and joy of our teacher, she was almost as small as us and when she played the piano she would have to take a pile of sheet music out of the stool to sit on so she could reach the keys. She was a nice teacher, but she did shout at us sometimes. Mollie never sat on the stool in case the teacher caught her. We had the classroom to ourselves because all the other children could go home for lunch. It was lovely sitting around the stove warming our toes and feeling full up. Mollie would stay with us until the other children were back and the teacher called us.

We used to go on nature walks, we didn't have far to go and would line up in twos in the playground and follow the teacher out into the lane, which eventually turned into a rough path. There was a little row of allotments on the right-hand side and a narrow path in-between two hedges, this path was our 'fields way home' I'll tell you more about that later, in the meantime we would follow the teacher a bit further to where the path opened up onto the football field, except that I don't remember ever seeing any goal posts or anything. Right at the bottom of the football field were some swings, a seesaw and some bars to play on, but on our nature walk we would have to stay near the path which had some really big trees and hedges and the teacher would tell us about the trees and the names, she would give us some paper and a pencil, which we would write our name on and draw round the leaves that we found on the ground. Sometimes she would ask us to go along the hedgerow and pick berries or flowers then she would look at what we had found and tell us the names. We would take them back to school and put them in jars of water. It's a good job our Mam didn't see us picking flowers, if she ever saw us she would always tell us off and say we must leave them to grow. She never changed her mind on that and would never have cut flowers in the house.

Every year we had a May Queen pageant and one little girl was chosen to be the May Queen and she would have a long white dress and flowers in her hair. All the other girls had daisy dresses and hats which were made of white crepe paper, and the hats had big white petals and the middle was yellow, so when you bent your head it looked like a big daisy and everyone had a garland of flowers. Not our Lionel though, boys didn't join in. The Butter Cross was all decked out with garlands twisted around the big stone pillars, at the top of the steps was a throne and a cloak and crown waiting for the Queen of the May, we were never chosen to be the May Queen, but we enjoyed being daises, or dancing around the Maypole platting the long, pretty-coloured ribbons.

Oh heck! I nearly forgot to tell you about the fields way home:

Well you see we went along the path between the hedges by the allotments and Mr Ludlam's field that always had this friendly horse in and he would see us coming along and waited for us at the gate to give him some grass from our hands, we always had some for him even though he had a field full so after spending a few moments rubbing his nose we would carry on until we came to the kissing gate that opened onto the cricket field, we would go right across to the other side, maybe stopping on the way to play by the pavilion, although we couldn't get in, it had steps up to a wooden platform with a rail along the front, and we liked stamping around on the boards and jumping off the steps, then on we would go to the far side of the field, where there was a narrow path between two very high walls which led out into Sunderland Street, by Stocks Meadow. We didn't go along there very often as it was very narrow and if someone was coming the other way you had a job to get past so we would just carry on into the next field, keeping to the back where there was a rough path, which I think we probably helped to make by using it so often. We would eventually come to the big, thick wall that was at the back of Vine Terrace, we would stretch up to try and grab the top of the wall, but it was very thick stone and it was hard for us to do so we sometimes gave each other a 'leg up' just to see if anyone was playing in the yard, sometimes Doreen would see her friend Lydia and they would have a chat, while we got fed up because we couldn't see anything. If we all got over the wall we could walk through to Sunderland Street and would be almost home as it brought us out near the little shop, you know the one that sold Grandad's shandy, but we liked to carry on along the field, as this bit was the best 'cos there were no high walls, we could see the farm and Sunderland Street, and it had a long down-hill run that we always did, and a stile to climb over into Common Lane, and then we were home.

Our mam didn't like us coming home this way, so we didn't always tell her, but sometimes she would know by the mud on our shoes.

One day at school the teacher told us that the next day we must come to school looking especially clean and tidy, with clean shoes and told not to play or dawdle on the way as tomorrow was going to be very special - a real princess was coming in a big car all the way from London - she was Princess Elizabeth - the King's daughter. Well we were so excited; we could hardly wait to tell our mam. The next day off we went to school looking very clean and tidy, we didn't dawdle and we didn't mess our hair up. Everyone in school was given a flag on a stick so that we could wave at the princess. We followed the teacher two by two down the lane into Sunderland Street where we were lined up along the edge of the pavement to wait for the car. I couldn't understand how everybody in the village was there and all the children from junior school had flags like ours and there were lots of flags on the Butter Cross and outside the shops as well, I thought that only our school knew about the princess coming.

Everyone was looking down Sunderland Street wanting to be the first to see the car, I suddenly thought, our mam will probably see the princess before we do as the car would be passing our house, maybe right this minute, then all of a sudden there were cars coming up the street towards us, everyone was cheering and waving their flags, so we did an all, I was waving and looking at all the cars and wondering if I had missed her, but then the biggest, shiniest car, with no top on came by, so, very slowly and there she was, the most beautiful princess of all and she was waving back. Then she was gone, but I just knew I would always remember seeing her. We followed the teacher two by two back up the lane to school, but the day seemed empty after that.

CHAPTER NINE

CHRISTMAS

Christmas was the time of year that our mam liked best of all. She was like a mother hen that gathered her brood close to her, making sure that none were missing. She would make a Christmas cake covered with icing that looked like snow and on the top would be Father Christmas, reindeers and a Christmas tree. She made Christmas pudding which we would all take a turn at stirring, for luck. When she put them into the pudding basins she would put a silver sixpence in and told us we would have to be very lucky to find it in the piece we got at Christmas dinner, Dad always said, he would find it first by making sure he got the right bit of pudding when it came to the table, I think Mam put a silver sixpence in every piece she served up, as we all got a sixpence, so did Dad. Whenever Mam was baking we always had the basin to run our fingers round until it was clean - we used to fight over that. We would have a fresh turkey from the farm that Mam would pluck herself. For tea there would be jelly and trifle, we liked them very much with Carnation milk poured over, jam tarts, mince pies, Bakewell tarts, sponge cake with jam and butter cream in, all made by our mam, pork pies, sausage rolls and lots of different sandwiches - cups of tea and lemonade.

On Christmas Eve we would have our bath, go up to bed and hang our stockings up on the bedpost, we were very excited, waiting for Father Christmas to call and leave a present for us. On Christmas morning in our stocking there would be an apple, orange, nuts and chocolate coins wrapped in gold paper and at the bottom of the bed wrapped up in Christmas paper we usually got something Kath, Millie and Margaret had knitted for us, sometimes we got handkerchiefs with embroidery in the corner, we always liked getting those not our Lionel though, he got socks and things and Snakes and Ladders or Ludo and that would mean that we would have to play for most of the afternoon with him. One year we had a great big rocking horse that we had to share, we didn't mind that - it was so big two of us could ride him at the same time. He wasn't new, Mam and Dad couldn't afford a new one as big as this - he didn't have rockers on but long sliding bars at each side. One of us could even stand on one of the bars while one sat on his back, we all thought he was great as he moved a long way forward and back, it was just like riding a real horse.

After tea we would play games like Musical Chairs, Pin The Tail On The Donkey and Pass The Parcel, we would run around and squeal until we were too tired to carry on. Mam would make us a hot drink and up to bed we would go, tired and happy. We loved Christmas time just as much as our mam did.

One Christmas Mam took the four of us to catch the bus, which would stop outside our house if we put our arm out to let the driver know we wanted to get on and we went to the village to see Auntie Annie and Uncle Harry, we had a little way to walk to their house when we got off the bus, along Castlegate and into Westgate. They had a terrace house in a row of four, they were made of shiny red bricks and I really liked touching them because they were so smooth, I think they were the only houses in the village that had shiny bricks like these. There was a gate at the side which opened onto a small backyard, every house had a door and window along the back and toilets for each house all in a row at the end of the yard, Auntie Annie's house was the last one, just outside her window she had a great big mangle with two huge wooden rollers and a big iron handle to turn them, which she used to wring out her washing.

She was a very big lady and she wasn't able to walk anywhere other than around the house or the yard, I think she was poorly and couldn't help being fat. Uncle Harry said that she used to be 'the fat lady' in a circus and would be away for months at a time but we didn't know if he was just kidding, then our mam said she did and that they dressed her as a fairy but Auntie Annie never minded and was always happy with the wages. She didn't have any children, she couldn't our mam said. Anyway when we got there we had some pop and home-made cake and mince pies and she gave us our Christmas presents, we stayed a little while then went off to get the bus home.

The bus stopped opposite our house, Mam always told us to wait until the bus had gone before we crossed the road, so that we could see both ways, anyway our Enid didn't want to wait, she wanted to be the first in to show her present so she ran round the back of the bus and just at the very same time an airforce lorry was coming the other way, it didn't see her and knocked her down. They jumped out, picked her up and took her into the house, she was shaking and crying and she had hurt her nose and her leg and she was to wear a calliper for quite a while. The next day the airmen called to see how Enid was, they made a big fuss of her and gave her a teddy bear, I must say our noses were pushed out.

I am eight and a half years old and the war is over. Everyone was happy and the street lights came on, not that it mattered very much to us as they didn't come down as far as our house, then they all started singing 'When the lights go on again all over the world.' I liked that song, our mam didn't put the black-out curtains up when it got dark, Dad said the war was over and that the big planes would not be coming over our house anymore. The Italian prisoners of war would be able to go back home to their families and I wondered if they really did have children like us waiting for them. All our soldiers, sailors and airmen would be happy to go home and I hoped this wouldn't take Arthur and Burt away as it would mean Kath and Millie wouldn't have a young man anymore. Sid would fetch Mollie and their children from our house - oh! I didn't want them to go.

We were going to have a street party. Our Enid went with Millie calling at all the big houses in Sunderland Street asking for donations, be it money or food for the party, and everyone was very generous, there were lots of flags and buntings waving across the street. There were long tables full with jellies, ice cream, cakes and sandwiches. All the grown-ups were dancing and singing and some of them were having a drink, I think our dad had a pint or two, and no wonder 'cos Mrs Spate was playing all the wartime songs on a piano in the street, we sang along with them an all but we just had lemonade and we were allowed to stay up late.

The soldiers that were billeted in Tickhill were all going home, maybe they would have a party like us.

CHAPTER TEN

SCARBOROUGH

Mam says we are all going on holiday to Scarborough, to a holiday camp. Mollie is going to look after Grandad while we are away as he hasn't been very well and stays in bed a lot now and our dad is going to join us a few days after we arrive at Scarborough. We were all very excited, we had never been on a holiday before, the thing is, the only Scarborough that I knew, was the pub that we passed on the way to school and I had never seen a holiday camp anywhere near there. Our mam got everything packed and a car came to take us, as we drove up Sunderland Street I remember thinking, we could have walked it, it's not that far to The Scarborough, but the car went straight by and I suddenly realised it wasn't that one at all, phew! I'm glad I hadn't said anything or I would have felt a bit daft, thinking we were having a holiday in The Scarborough Arms pub, the car, in fact was taking us to Doncaster train station, we had never been on a train before either.

Hooray! The seaside.

Scarborough was lovely, the beach has lots of little rock pools on it, we had fishing nets and caught teeny weenie crabs but we put them back, sometimes we took them to another pool that didn't have any and popped them in, to give them a change, it was a lovely sandy beach with some great big rocks sticking out, big enough for us to sit on, which we did a lot.

The holiday camp where we were staying was very high up from the beach, we had a sort of cabin, with a kitchen, living room and bedrooms, but there was no water tap, just outside there was a big green where we could play games and on the edge of this was a water tap, a place to wash and a toilet but we didn't mind that, it was not much further away than our toilet at home.

When we were not at the beach, we played rounders or cricket. Our Lionel had a cricket bat you see, so we did our best.

One morning we got up and Mam said our dad would be coming today, so we played on the grass all the time looking out for him. We seemed to have been playing for ages, then at last there he was, walking across the green, we all ran as fast as our legs could carry us to meet him, shouting to Mam, 'Dad's here, Dad's here,' Oh it was nice to have him with us. Later, we all went down to the beach, we couldn't wait to show our dad the rock pools, with the crabs in, which by the way, were now 'our crabs'.

It seemed that Dad had only been with us for a day or two when a telegram came from Mollie, to say that Grandad had died. Our mam was crying, I'd never seen her cry before, she said we must all go home and I thought oh Grandad why did you have to go and die just when we were having a lovely holiday. I didn't say anything to Mam, because she would have cried again and it frightened me when she cried.

We all went home.

CHAPTER ELEVEN
MILLIE'S WEDDING

It's Christmas time and our Millie is getting married to her airman, Arthur, she's having lots and lots of bridesmaids, including all of us. Our Kath and Margaret will be her big bridesmaids then our Doreen, Enid and me will be her little ones and her really tiny one with be Gloria, Mickey will be her page boy, not our Lionel though, 'cos he's too tall. She is getting married in St Mary's Church, you know the big one in the village.

We couldn't believe that we were going to be bridesmaids we had never been to a wedding before, never mind being bridesmaids. Doreen, Enid and me are having pink dresses - all the same, Kath and Margaret will be different, little Gloria's dress will be the same as mine - pink, Mickey is to have short velvet trousers and a frilly blouse, good job Lionel wasn't a page boy, I don't think they would have got him into a frilly blouse or velvet trousers - even though he still wore short trousers. We liked it when we had to try on our dresses, I'm sure we must have told everyone we saw about it.

The day had come and we were bubbling over with excitement, we had been bathed the night before, you know, the bath night routine except we didn't have rags in our hair because today we were going to have it tonged, so here we were in the front room, the one Grandad used to have, there was a nice fire burning in the grate, our dresses were all hanging up, Kath and Margaret were heating up the curling tongs, which I for one didn't like the look of. They were putting them into the fire and they had some old newspaper they would use to test the heat of the tongs. If they scorched the paper they had to wait a while and test again until it was cool enough to use on our hair. We were all moaning, saying it was burning us and pulling our hair, oh I wish my hair didn't get pulled so much, Gloria was lucky that day because she had lovely curls all over her head, but not so lucky the day she got sticky buds in them. There was another little girl in the room with us, I think she must have come with Auntie Hetty and Uncle Frank from Warsop, she was going to be a bridesmaid too, she was about the same age as our Enid and will have a pink dress as well.

Outside the snow was falling and it was freezing cold, but it didn't bother us, we were now all dressed and ready to go, I hadn't seen our Millie all morning, she must be upstairs, getting ready. I hadn't seen her dress or anything and I don't know where our Lionel is either but I can't worry about that now, I'm sure he'll turn up somewhere soon, that's what our mam used to say when we had lost something 'Don't worry it will turn up somewhere soon,' and it usually did.

The car had arrived to take us to the church, our Kath and Margaret in charge of us, the snow was coming down quite heavy now but with the help of the driver we were in the car in no time at all and off we went up Sunderland Street hoping that someone we knew would see us in the posh car with our lovely frocks on.

The church was cold after the warm car ride, there were lots of people already in the church sitting quietly in the pews and sort of whispering to each other while they waited for the bride, at last here she was, our Millie. Oh! She was so lovely in her white wedding dress and veil, I just kept on looking at her and Uncle Frank was holding her arm, so that's why he came, oh, the things I have to work out for myself, nobody tells me anything. Our Kath and Margaret were doing their best to get us into some kind of order, with Mickey first, holding Millie's train, then Gloria, our Enid, and our new friend from Warsop, then me and our Doreen, two by two behind them, with Kath and Margaret bringing up the rear.

The organ started to play and Uncle Frank walked our Millie down the long aisle with the rest of us following behind walking past family, friends and neighbours. Oh! There's our Lionel, looking smart, and he has taken his cap off, I bet our mam told him not to forget to do that; anyway he'd 'turned up'. Come to think of it I had not seen much of our mam so far, I wonder if she is in church or getting on with things at home, maybe I'll spot her soon.

Mr Cook, the vicar of the parish was a tall man with a big, deep, booming voice and he married Millie and Arthur. After the service was over, we had gone into the little room just by the alter so that Millie and Arthur could sign the register, apparently everyone who gets married has to do it. Our Kath and Margaret were trying once again to get us in order before we walked back up the aisle to the great big doors at the end. They were now open and we could hear the bells ringing out for them. We couldn't have our photographs taken because the snow was still falling and it was quite deep and very, very cold. I thought it was a shame not to have any photos taken especially as we all looked so nice in our frocks and things.

The reception was in the parish room; there were lots of long tables and a big wedding cake that had three tiers and a little bride and groom on the top. People were making speeches and laughing and Millie and Arthur gave all the bridesmaids a present, I didn't know that bridesmaids got presents, so that was something else I wasn't told. I loved mine, it was a bracelet with yellow beads dotted here and there all around it, our mam said I mustn't play in the garden or go to bed with it on, so I used to wear it mostly on Sundays. We went to bed very late that night, no peeping through the curtains to see them kissing goodnight anymore, but we decided that we could still look out for our Kath and Margaret, couldn't we!

It was about a week later that we were once again in the front room having our hair tonged, trying not to complain about the heat or our hair being pulled. What was happening was that we were all going to a photographer to have wedding photos take in his studio. We were all back in our posh frocks, our Millie in her wedding dress and Arthur was looking smart in his uniform. The snow was still falling, I don't think it had stopped since the wedding; it was so thick on the ground that Arthur had to carry us to the car. He looked funny all dressed up with very wet feet.

Every Christmas after that, we asked our Millie to put the record, I'm Dreaming Of A White Christmas on her gramophone, we liked this gramophone it had a handle that you had to wind up tight before putting the needle arm on the record 'cos if you forgot the music would get slower and slower and the singer singing deeper and deeper and made everyone laugh but not as much as when we saw Arthur holding his ears and shouting 'Turn it off, turn it off! I don't want to be reminded of a white Christmas, not after carrying bridesmaids to and from cars, let alone the bride,' and he would chase us around the house, we never got tired of doing that to him, year after year after year.

CHAPTER TWELVE

CASTLEGATE

We are moving house!

Number one Castlegate. It is in the centre of the village, next door to the library, which had nice wide steps leading up to the big door, but there were no books in it so I don't know why they called it that. Mam said the house would have to be cleaned thoroughly, all the walls needed to be white-washed, floors scrubbed and windows cleaned. The first time we saw it was when we went with Kath, Margaret and Millie and as Millie still didn't have a baby to put in her big cream pram, it was filled with packets and bottles of cleaning stuff and some pop for us to drink.

This house is very big. If you look at it from the other side of the road, it is built with large grey stones; the front is taken up by lots of windows. The ground floor has a stone arch, which leads to the side door and along the front is a large shop window and door then a smaller window. The next floor has four windows across, one of them being above the arch, at the very top, the attic, has three windows. It must have been a coach house a long time ago when coach and horses were used. There were more of these arches in Tickhill, The Red Lion, the pub opposite has a big arch and so has The Three Crowns that is near the parish room. Our mam told us that some of the soldiers who were billeted in Tickhill during the war used this house and now we were going to live in it. We couldn't believe how big it was, it had electricity, plus a toilet with a water flush and can you believe, it's just across the yard, hurrah! So, what with the village centre, the short walk to school and electricity we had found our waterloo, what? Let me tell you, we were right made up!

We didn't know what to explore first, the inside or out.

We went into the house through the side door in the courtyard which had a stone pump trough under the living room window, but it didn't pump water anymore. There was a water tap in the living room with a large shallow stone sink and the biggest Yorkshire range I had ever seen. There would be times later on when I wished it had been a lot smaller. It had two water boilers, one each side, that would give lots of room for Mam to put pots, pans and kettles to keep warm and a large oven. There was a small high window at the back that looked out onto the library - as we went through the side door, there was a square with a red tiled floor. We helped to take all the cleaning stuff out of the pram, then asked if we could go and look around, they said we could, but not to open any windows, and to be careful. We were off like a shot.

We went back out of the living room to the red tiled square hall where there was a door to the pantry that had stone shelves and a tiny window at the back. It was very cold in there, which would be good for Mam to keep food fresh. There was a passage leading off the square and it had a door into a little room with a fireplace and a small window, also looking out onto the library, the passage now opened up into another square with a big window looking out onto the courtyard and ahead were two steps up to a door with a large wall cupboard to the right of it. This door led into the shop, and on the right, another led into a large front room with a lovely fireplace and a nice big window. Retracing our steps back to the living room we found a staircase in the passage, it had two stairs that curled round, then it went straight up. At the top of this flight of stairs was a large landing, with two tiny bedrooms along a narrow landing with a balustrade along so you didn't fall onto the stairs below, both had tiny windows the far one had an inner wall with a large square right in the middle, but no door, we poked our heads in, it was a kind of storage space. We spotted two very large bibles bound in leather with gilt clasps to close them, when we told Mam later she said we would just leave them there for the time being. Back on the landing another flight of five steps with banisters either side, led to a long landing that went from left to right of you. To the right there was a door at the end, opening onto a lovely bedroom with a fireplace and a large window looking out onto Castlegate, going back past the head of the stairs was another bedroom much the same as the one we had just seen except this one was bigger and had two windows, at the end of the landing were three steps leading up onto a small square, straight ahead was another bedroom but this one was over the stone arch and had a window at the front and back, we liked this one the best, when we looked out of the back window we could see just how big the yard was - we must hurry to see the rest of the inside in case it was time to go home before we had seen everything. Back on the tiny landing was a door and when we opened this, there was yet another flight of stairs - these were narrower than the others we had climbed and closed in by a wall on each side, we were beginning to wonder how many more we would find. It was getting a bit spooky but we carried on and found the best attic you could ever wish for. It was a large room that covered the entire house, the three windows were not as big and square as the others we had seen, but when we looked down it was a long way to the ground. We could see the top of St Mary's Church if we looked straight out, then right in the corner guess what? more stairs, just five of them leading to the teeniest room we had ever seen, with another of those very small windows that looked out onto the library.

It was such a big house with so many rooms, but I was in no doubt that me mam would fill them in no time at all. We went back down to the living room where Kath, Millie and Margaret were busy cleaning, had a quick drink of pop and asked if we could go outside, once again they agreed, but not to go onto the road and to be careful, we all shouted that we would and raced out into the courtyard. We didn't know where to start, it seemed there was so much to explore.

As we stepped out of the door looking across the courtyard was the 'water loo' there was a little window high up in the wall just to the right of it, which we found out later was our neighbours Mr and Mrs Bradder's living room window, they were about the same age as our mam and dad. The wall continued at the other side of the toilet door, this was a long low building with windows along the front looking onto the courtyard, there was lots of space in here, with a long bench underneath the windows, and a funny little wall at the end where the door was, with a gap each side, so you could go in at one end and out the other, our Lionel said it might have been a slaughter house, just the thought of it made us squeal and run out holding our dresses tight around our legs as though something would catch hold of us and slaughter us, our Lionel thought it was funny when he frightened us. Joined onto this was a wash house, it had a big brick built copper just inside the door with a fire grate underneath, it wasn't very wide and had one small window, Mam would like this, she could boil lots of clothes in it.

On the opposite side, attached to the house was another building again with a large window and door at the front and lots of space inside, attached to this was a smaller one. The courtyard finished here. Now we were in a large open yard on rough ground. Looking down we could see a large stone barn, which we would get to eventually, but right now on our left-hand side, was a high stone wall that separated us from the ground behind the library, this was very thick and high, too high for us to climb, even grown-ups would have a bit of a job trying to get over this wall. On the right-hand side the wash house wall made a nice place to play ball, with a lower wall that separated us from Mr and Mrs Bradder's garden along the side. Then there was a granary with big uneven steps going up to the door where the grain would have been kept, a bit like the one at the Mill Dam, we were told never to climb the steps as they were too dangerous so although we were tempted from time to time we never saw inside. Then the yard became wider, with two small stables built onto the side of the granary looking onto quite a big square, the back part of which had a square of concrete, we thought there must have been some sort of building there at one time, just behind this the old grey stone wall ran along the back which was too high to see over with yet another door, this one was a bit hard to get open, but our Lionel managed to open it - we couldn't believe it, here was an orchard, it had pear trees and lots and lots of very high nettles, so we couldn't go in too far. We agreed to sort that out another day, so we closed the door and walked around the side of what we found to be the great big barn with two wooden doors, one of which was partly open, so with Lionel going first we managed to get inside, it was huge - absolutely loads and loads of space and a loft, which reminded us all of Walter, we couldn't help laughing, after spending some time in here looking to see if there was anything that would be of use to us, you know like old pram wheels or bits of wood, we squeezed back out of the doors and went to look into the last door which was attached the barn and the other side joined the high stone wall that separated us from the library, it was another stable, but this one would hold three horses, there was a manger along the wall attached to the barn with a big iron cradle to hold the hay, Lionel said he would climb into the manger first and see what was up there. He thought there might be some hay but we were already scrambling into it further down so there were four heads poking through having a neb, but there wasn't, shame it would have been nice to have a hay fight but, with Walter in mind, certainly not up there.

That was our exploring done and we decided that we were going to like living here. Now we were eager to get home and tell Mam and Dad all that we had seen.

CHAPTER THIRTEEN

MOVING IN

I knew I was right! It didn't take long for Mam to fill the house; in fact in no time at all it was full to busting!

Kath and Bert were planning to get married and lived with us - Millie and Arthur came, Margaret too and Uncle Jim, Mam's brother came with us an' all, he was just like our Lionel, tall and thin except he didn't wear glasses. Cyril stayed for a little while, then went away to work at Butlins Holiday Camp which had not long opened in Skegness, and came home every now and then. Auntie Annie had died, I did say she was poorly, we were not told at the time, that - what they don't know won't hurt them thing again. Uncle Harry must have stayed on in the house with the shiny red bricks and eventually met, whom we now know as Auntie Peggy, she wasn't a very tall lady, her hair was cut much the same as our own except she didn't have a fringe and she always wore a nice hair slide to hold it back, so Auntie Peggy and Uncle Harry came to live with us too, they had the little room along the passage, off the red tiled square hall for their private living room, which Auntie Peggy made really comfy, with a fire in the grate on cold days - there was a table to eat off and Auntie Peggy could always pop whatever she had prepared to cook, in the Yorkshire range oven. Sometimes if we smelt something nice, like home-baked bread, we would soon call to say hello, then get hot bread and butter, we liked Auntie Peggy's home-baked bread and we loved having our Uncle Harry close by us. The Yorkshire range was shiny black after being cleaned, a big fire was burning and warmed the whole room, it had a fender with a brass rail around and a companion set with long brass handles and a high sturdy fireguard surrounding it all. Inside the door the sink was to the left, by the big window, the one with the pump trough underneath; the Yorkshire range opposite the door and in the corner by the window, a large cupboard from the floor almost to the ceiling. That left enough space for our Lionel to keep the white mice that he managed to persuade Mam to let him have, he kept them in a shoe box. When he got them down to feed and clean we would jump on a chair holding onto our skirts until he put them back, he was always frightening us, even pretending they were on the floor sometimes. These were to be the first of many pets he had while we were at Castlegate. At the other side of the fireplace is Dad's wooden armchair; it opened out into a single bed, which was rarely used. It had two big cushions on the back and seat and looked very comfy, only Dad sat in it and after dinner he would nod off to sleep. He did this on a Saturday afternoon as well, when he listened to football on his wireless - our Dad liked football, he used to be a linesman for Tickhill Rovers - he always made sure that the accumulator was full - he had two of these contraptions, one, in use in the wireless and the other being charged up at the little shop a few doors away. We would often call at the shop for the full one, these things were about the size of a house brick but square and much heavier, they had liquid sealed inside and there was a swinging handle to carry them, this cut into your fingers with the sheer weight of the thing, so anyway, there would be Dad laying back in his armchair with his eyes

70

closed and the football commentator shouting out every move the players made, we would get home sometimes and thinking he was asleep, creep by him and turn the little knob on the wireless to another station, but he was never really asleep and would make us jump saying 'Leave that alone you little buggers,' without even opening his eyes and we would have to tune it back to the football. We were all kinds of buggers, clever, bad, daft, cheeky and silly. At the other end of the room was a big, wooden table, the one the bath used to stand on when we were in Sunderland Street, along the wall behind it was a black, horse hair chaise longue 'sofa' it was very hard, very uncomfortable and the horse hair used to stick in our legs and bums, especially in the summer when we wore thin cotton dresses. Not our Lionel though, he wore trousers but he had to make sure they were long enough so his legs didn't get itchy - he was still in short ones you see but, if he loosened his braces he could pull his trousers down a bit before he sat down and that would make things better for him, there were also some heavy wooden chairs at the table. We didn't have to call at Rawson's farm for the milk after school anymore because Mr Shipley of Friary Farm, Rotherham Road came along Castlegate every morning with his horse and cart that had huge milk churns in, so all we had to do was take the big milk jugs from the pantry and he would ladle the milk in - very handy - then we put them straight back into the pantry.

As you know we had electricity and the only plug that I can remember was the one under the tiny window at the back of the living room. Audrey, a friend of our Kath's bought Mam an electric kettle, which pleased Mam - because Dad would be able to use it to make his early morning tea instead of waiting for the kettle to boil on the fire. The only place she could put it was in the high little window at the back of the room, 'A bit dangerous.' Mam said, so we were told that we must never plug the kettle in. Bath nights were not the same anymore, sometimes we went to Audrey's for a bath and Mam paid her in kind with coal, we liked bathing in a big bath that had taps, one of which had hot water, it wasn't too far for us to go, she lived with her family in King Edward Road at the other side of the church, but mostly we filled the copper with water, lit the fire underneath and in the meantime took the long zinc bath from the wash house to our water loo - now what I didn't tell you before was - this was the biggest loo anyone had ever seen, it was so long you could form a queue inside and what's more it was always nice and warm thanks to Mrs Bradder's fire which backed on to the long side wall and like our Mam's never went out. While the water in the copper got hot we fetched soap, towels and night-gowns and slippers from our bedroom then filled the bath with hot water carrying it by the bucketful. The big, wooden door on the loo had a heavy iron latch and just underneath, a round hole as big as a penny that we bunged up with paper. There were always two of us in the loo bathing and when one of us got out to dry and jump into a night-gown the next one came in usually with a bucket full of hot water for the bath. When we were all done we got as much water as we could out with a bucket then lifted the bath into the courtyard and poured the rest into the little, square drain which was in the middle - our mam said it was there so the rain water could run away otherwise we would have big puddles everywhere.

Mrs Crossland, who lived near Vine Terrace - the lady Mam used to worry about had lost her husband, now Mam was even more worried so, Mrs Crossland came to live with us an all, she was a really nice lady, short and plump. She loved Mrs Dale's Diary and would listen to it every day on Dad's wireless at just about the time that we would be home from school - we used to listen to Dick Barton, Special Agent, he was on at seven o'clock some nights, we would always make sure we were home in good time to listen, it was a serial you see so we didn't like missing any - a bit like Mrs Crossland. Mam would 'Shush' us as we came in the door so as not to disturb her. I remember one day when we came home Mrs Crossland was listening to the wireless as usual and she was in tears, apparently one of the characters on Mrs Dale's Diary had died, our Dad pulled her leg, the way he did when we watched Roy Rogers, and that soon made her laugh, which was good to see as she still went to the churchyard every day to sit by her husband's grave and she would talk to him. Sometimes our mam would send one of us to look for her and bring her back home, she was a dear little lady and I am glad that Mam brought her to live with us, except, with all this going on it was taking its toll on our mam. She had put on quite a lot of weight, simply because she could not move around without holding on to the furniture, you see her leg was now ulcerated and swollen and she was in a great deal of pain.

But what gave her more pain and heartache was the fact that our Kath was very poorly, she had tuberculosis, 'consumption of the lungs.' We all had to have a test at a clinic in Doncaster, where we had a little patch stuck on our back, then we went back the following week for the results. All four of us were clear. I'm sure Mam and Dad breathed a sigh of relief. Kath had to have her own cutlery and crockery, but through all this she stayed cheerful, determined to get better and was looking forward to marrying Bert. When Mam and Dad realised just how poorly she was, Dad tried to dissuade Bert from marrying her at this time, making sure that he knew just how poorly she was, but he didn't listen. Our Kath had a lovely white wedding; she was married in Tickhill Church, with Dad, sad but proud, walking by her side down the aisle to give her away. This was the last thing on earth he wanted to do. Mam and Dad were not at all keen on Bert, he was tall and thin with dark hair, Dad called him a 'Brillcreem boy', that's what everyone called the boys in the RAF. Bert was very moody and sulky, he would sit in the corner of the room with the newspaper in front of his face, not even reading it. He didn't try to get a job or make conversation with any of us; maybe he was at a loss after the war and leaving the air force.

They had the lovely big attic to live in after they were married; a partition was put up so that they had a sitting room and bedroom. Kath made it really nice and cosy and all the lovely wedding presents were put to use. It wasn't long before Dad found out that Bert had been hitting her at night because she used to cough and disturb him. Dad took him to task about it and he got so angry that he picked up the long poker from the hearth and chased him out of the house, telling him never to set foot inside the door again. Everyone was upset, our Kath most of all, she didn't deserve this, she was the sweetest kindest person in the whole world, she really was.

Bert would write to her regularly asking her to go to him, he lived near Bristol which was a long way from home, eventually she gave in and went, nothing Mam or Dad said could change her mind. She wrote home regularly giving them her news, hoping they were not worrying too much about her. Then the letter came telling them, she wanted to come home, she was poorly and very unhappy, she wrote 'I have no money, please send my train fare or I shall start walking home.' Dad didn't waste any time in sending her the fare and she was back home in no time at all, exhausted and very poorly.

The doctor came to visit her at home and said she needed to be in hospital, as tuberculosis is a very infectious disease Kath was taken to a sanatorium, a hospital for tubercular patients, it was at Knaresborough in North Yorkshire. She wrote a long letter home every week telling us all about it, she said all the wards were facing gardens and had a veranda, every day come rain or shine the windows and sliding glass doors would be opened and all the beds would be pushed on to the veranda, even when the snow was falling the beds were pushed out, every bed had its own special, yellow, oil-skin bed cover to keep the blankets dry. She wrote about the birds that came down onto the lawns for food, the friends she had made and walked with through the grounds of the sanatorium. Our dad spent every Sunday with her and he took us to see her once. There was no known cure, no drugs to make her better, Kath's letters lost their sparkle; she was unhappy and home-sick. A few weeks later she wrote that the doctors wanted to operate on her lung and she was frightened as one of her friends had a similar operation and had died. She wanted to come home, she pleaded with Dad when he visited - how could he refuse - it was agreed that she could leave on condition that she did not sleep in the house and it would be arranged for a special hut to be put up outside. They came to inspect the grounds for a suitable spot for the hut and decided that the concrete square by the orchard door would be the perfect spot. Mam wasn't at all happy about it - it was so far away from the house - but when Kath was told, she said she would be alright sleeping down there. The hut was big enough for a single bed and side cupboard, there were no windows, just oil-skin shutters all the way round that had to be opened when she was sleeping, there was also a yellow, oil-skin cover for her bed. Mam was almost out of her mind with worry. She sent for the local bobby and asked if it would be possible for the night duty officer to patrol the yard and he gladly agreed and promised it would be done every night, top priority which made her feel a little better.

Our Kath came home to us, she was oh so brave and we were glad to have her back.

CHAPTER FOURTEEN

THE SHOP

Mr Fanthorpe who lived by the church gate in Tickhill called on Mam one day to ask if she was going to use the shop - if not he would like to rent it to sell fruit, vegetables and wet fish. They came to an agreement and Mam gave him the keys to the shop door at the front. It didn't take long before he put up a partition, so that we could get into our front room without going into the shop, when we now used the door at the end of the red brick hall, we found a small square and our room was on the right. He furnished the shop with a counter, shelves and had a nice window display for his fish and the shop got off to a flying start. He had a horse and dray and would bring it round to the front of the shop to load it, then take his wares around the village one or two days a week.

Dad had brought a Yorkshire terrier home for us and he was a little rascal, we called him Paddy, Doreen loved him, - she loved all animals and let him sleep in bed with her, that would be alright normally but I shared the bed with her and I wasn't too keen, if we moved in bed he would growl at us, he usually spent all night by our feet, and as I couldnt' sleep all night without moving, I usually got growled at a lot, Doreen just laughed at him. Well I put up with this because I knew Doreen would be upset if I told her I didn't want him in the bed. He must have seen Mr Fanthorpe's horse at some time when we had taken him out on his lead - he had to have a lead or he would be off all over the place. He seemed to know whenever the horse was outside and he would do all he could to get out of the door - now that wasn't too hard for him, because, everyone was coming in and out all day long. Mam used to say 'That bloody door is opening and closing from dawn till dusk.' Because it was never locked through the day it was a piece of cake to him. He would bide his time then make a dart for the door the minute someone came through it and before our mam could call 'Don't let Paddy out' he was already racing under the arch, barking and snapping at the horse's legs, setting it off up Castlegate with Mr Fanthorpe running behind trying to catch the horse, Paddy, thinking this was good fun would snap at Mr Fanthorpe's heels too. Sometimes Mr Fanthorpe would manage to catch the horse's reins before Paddy set him off. This would happen reguarly, even though we did our very best to keep him in. Mr Fanthorpe would even let us know when the horse would be there, so we could be extra vigilant. I think Paddy knew what he was saying and made an extra effort to get out.

The best thing about Paddy - he was a good guard dog for our Kath, when she slept in the hut she would often take him with her and I must say good for me too as I could go to sleep and move about as much as I liked - Doreen would much rather have had Paddy growling than me tossing and turning all night and I think the local bobby would have preferred Paddy in the house rather than come face to face with him at the bottom of the yard in the middle of the night but that didn't last long as Mam couldn't rest knowing Kath was down there on her own and soon had her sleeping in the house again.

One morning in school the teacher told us we were going to the library in the afternoon for a lecture on road safety followed by a film. We were all looking forward to this, at least it would be a change from being in the classroom and just next door to our house would mean we would be home quicker. When everyone was settled down the lecture began, it was a bit boring as we were being told all the things that Mam had told us anyway, look both ways before crossing the road, don't play ball in the road, if you own a dog be sure to keep in on a lead, stuff like that. We were glad when the film started, but that looked like being boring too, as it was now showing us, crossing the road without looking, then it went on to show pets behaving badly. We couldn't believe it when we realised that Paddy was the pet on the film, we almost shouted out 'Oh look, it's our Paddy!' But stopped just in time when we saw he was not on his lead, but causing havoc, running here and there barking at everything he saw, running across the road and back - he was at his worst - showing us up, that's what he was doing, I would have liked to crawl under my chair. We burst through the door when we got home and told Mam, she was not amused, in fact this was the last straw and we were told in no uncertain terms that, what with Mr Fanthorpe's horse and now this a new home would have to be found for Paddy. This started our Doreen off crying, saying she would make sure it didn't happen again but Mam would not be moved and a few weeks later Derek, a relative of ours from outside the village collected him and took him home with him. It was about four weeks later that Doreen went to see how he was getting on - Mam told her not to fetch him home with her or else, Doreen came home without Paddy - upset - she told Mam he was all dirty and thin and he was so pleased to see her that he couldn't possibly be happy, Mam told her she was a 'balm pot' and not to be so daft. We didn't see him again but I'm sure he was happy there.

We had just got settled into our new home when the war came flooding back, a tank being transported on a low-loader was turning by Snell's shop, out of Sunderland Street into Castlegate when the tank slipped almost falling off, the soldiers travelling with it deciding to get help would have a long wait and on hearing this Mam sent us out to offer them a cup of tea so before we knew it they were in the courtyard having tea and some of our Mam's home-made cake, it took an awful long time before they were on their way again, they thanked Mam and we waved them goodbye, that was the last time we saw any soldiers in Tickhill.

It was the first Christmas that we had spent in Castlegate, our shared present was a toy sweet shop, we set it out in the red, tiled, square hall, it was made of cardboard and when it was opened out, had a counter, a till with cardboard coins and weighing scales, little tins of pretend soup, beans, peas, tiny boxes of cornflakes, bags of sugar and little jars of real Dolly Mixtures, which quickly became the best selling item and the shop soon sold out of them, the next day when we set it up it wasn't much fun because there were no sweets, I don't know who said what, to start with, but we all decided we would go across the road to the sweet shop and take a handful of sweets, just enough to fill the jars and that is just what we did, so with the jars full we started to play -

buying the sweets as fast as we could. Our mam came out of the living room on her way to the pantry just behind us and stopped in her tracks, calling out, 'Where did you get those sweets from?' we said they came with the shop, 'Oh no,' Mam said, 'You have already eaten those, now tell me the truth,' and we did, she got a paper bag, emptied what sweets were left into it and took us out onto the pavement, she gave us the bag saying she would wait by the arch while we took them back and said sorry, we were crying and begging her not to send us but she would have none of it and nudged us to the edge of the pavement - crying and with our tails between our legs we went. When we got back to her she said 'That will teach you not to steal again.' And she was right, it was a hard lesson we learned that day but we never stole again.

CHAPTER FIFTEEN

JUNIOR SCHOOL

Things were much the same as they were in Sunderland Street, we still went to Sunday school and as we got older we went in the evenings to the big chapel and sat in the pews upstairs, they all had a low door at the side, some holding four or more people and some just for two. We still went on the trips to the seaside getting our paper hats as soon as we got off the coach and we bought a small present between us for our mam, she didn't get many presents. Mam used to organise coach trips herself, always using the same company to book the coach and we usually had the same driver every time, it was mostly our family and a few friends and neighbours that went and everybody sang songs on the way to the seaside and sang the same ones on the way home but much louder, we loved going on our mam's coach trips.

On Mother's Day we would scramble over the castle wall to pick some violets from the banks of the moat for her, she always said thank you before telling us not to pick them any more as they liked growing in the wild. We used to do errands for Mam at the grocery shop just over the road and we saw a big, brown teapot like the one Mam used and as it was not far away from Mother's Day, the lady said she would put it by for us and let us pay some of our pocket money every week - a bit like our mam did. Every week she would have Mr Clayton's book ready for him when he called along with what ever money she could afford to pay, he came every week and just knocked on the door calling 'It's only me Mrs

Cooper' as he walked into the living room, he was ever so nice and always stayed long enough for a chat with Mam and before going said 'Do you need anything this week Mrs Cooper?' and if we needed new clothes he would take our sizes and bring them with him the following week. We liked to see Mr Clayton 'cos if we were playing in the yard he always waved calling hello to us and if we knew he had something for us to try on we would be through the door right behind him, our mam said he was a god send as there were no shops in Tickhill that sold clothes - anyway that's what we did, and our mam had a lovely, big, brown teapot for Mother's Day instead of violets. Mam was really surprised and pleased with us for keeping it a secret.

We went to the junior school that was just by the church, it was much bigger than the infant school house, with more classrooms and a huge playground and the boys used to play football in the field behind. Mam always inspected us before we went to school and when she was satisfied we were clean and tidy and saying 'You'll do' gave us a few coppers before sending us off, our first stop would be the baker's shop just across the road it was the last shop almost opposite the parish room and just the smell of the freshly baked bread would have us lingering around outside, looking in the window trying to decide what to spend our pennies on, our favourites were, a warm bread cake or tea cake they were straight out of the oven and we couldn't' resist them - bit like Auntie Peggy's bread - then we made our way to school, we didn't need to go all the way back to Church Lane 'cos there was Drury Lane - a sort of alley -

between the shops we had passed on our way to the baker's which was a really good short cut, it had a high wall each side - like the one in Sunderland Street but this one had a funny squiggly bend at the beginning then straight all the way to the lane right by our school, we sometimes came this way home an all especially if we still had enough money to call in at the baker's, plus, we liked racing through shouting our heads off all the way into Castlegate as our voices sort of echoed, everyone liked doing this. We came this way to get to the library - the one that had no books - for school dinners but the teacher was with us then so we didn't shout our heads off. We would much rather have gone home for something to eat but we knew we had better not because when we told Mam we didn't like them, especially the cabbage, she said, 'Well you are going because they are good for you and that's that!'

The thing that was even worse than school dinners was the dentist that visited the school, just the sight of that big, ugly chair being taken into the classroom that stood on its own in the playground, frightened me half to death, when everything was set up, one class at a time had to line up outside to be called in one by one, oh the thought of sitting in that chair, it's a wonder I didn't wet my knickers.

There were some naughty boys in my class and the teacher who was a little, thin man was always calling one or the other out to the front of the class to give them the cane, they would hold their hand out - it never seemed to bother them but the poor teacher would be hopping mad and sometimes the cane would break and the teacher would throw it to the floor telling the boy to fetch another one with him tomorrow, then march off to his desk, plonk himself down on his chair and would sit, elbows on the desk pushing his hands through his hair until he had calmed down and I felt sorry for our teacher.

I remember a little boy called Billie, he was in our Enid's class and lived just across the lane from the school, he wasn't able to learn as quickly as the rest of us and when the school bell rang for home time his mam was always waiting by the front gate and Billie would run into her open arms, some of the boys used to tease him and call him Silly Billie, our mam said they were wicked children and if she ever heard that we had called him names we would get a smacked arse.

Dad still mended our shoes, he had a bench by the window in the coal house, where he kept his 'tackle' that's what he called the things he needed to do jobs, if it was a nice, warm day he would take his 'tackle' out onto the yard to cobble our shoes. He still cut our hair, he did this in the red, tiled square that had the window, he kept his barber's 'tackle' in a square biscuit tin in the big cupboard in the living room, we had the same as always, Lionel a short back and sides, Doreen, Enid and me, a fringe, the rest cut straight across the bottom just below our ears, as we sat in the chair we always asked Dad not to cut it too short but he ignored us and throwing the sheet around our shoulders telling us to sit still - which we always did anyway 'cos if we didn't he would tap us none to gently on the top of our heads with the comb, so we stretched our necks to make them as long as possible in the hope that when we relaxed, our hair would look longer, Dad must have spotted what we were up to and took it into account as it never worked for us, now and again we would ask him if we could grow our hair really long, but it was always the same answer 'I'll have to ask mother.' When we asked Mam she said 'I'll speak to your father.' We were getting nowhere, but we kept on trying.

I was getting sore throats and feeling poorly and the doctor said I needed my tonsils out and arranged for me to go into Doncaster Infirmary. I was really frightened when the day came for me to go but our Kath took me to the hospital reassuring me that everything would be alright and I would be back home in no time at all but I cried and didn't want her to leave me, she stayed by me as long as she could until the nurse said she must go. The next day I woke up to be told I could not have anything to eat or drink and the nurse put me in a funny gown - nothing like my familiar wincyette nightie that Mam had packed for me. There were other children in the ward and they had to wear the funny gowns an all, then we were all taken into a long, narrow room and sat side by side on the wooden bench along the wall. We all had a big, red blanket around our shoulders and that scared me 'cos I thought we had them round us so we wouldn't see all the blood when they took our tonsils out. One by one the nurse took us out of the room - I had never been so scared in all my life as I was sitting on that bench with the red blanket wrapped around me.

I had a sore throat and found it hard to swallow when I woke up but then the nice bit came when the nurse told me that only thing I could have to eat was ice cream, then I thought well, I could go home and me mam could give me some ice cream so why doesn't our Kath come to fetch me? But she didn't, that is not until the following day when she took me home and I told everyone how brave I was and how it didn't hurt, not even mentioning the red blanket.

CHAPTER SIXTEEN

PLAYTIME

Our mam said we must always come home from school first and have our tea and change our clothes before going out to play or we would get our arses smacked, so we did. It was nice being able to have our friends to play - we could call for them, because we were a bit more grown-up now and they didn't have so far to walk to our house, our Lionel was always out with his friends and they came to play in our yard as well, there was plenty of space for them to play football or cricket, he would often get us to make the numbers up and would put us in goal or fielding if they were playing cricket. We always got fed-up after a little while and when we didn't want to play anymore he called us 'mardy buggers', we didn't care what he called us as long as we got away. We liked skipping which we did on the square piece of concrete by the orchard door or in the courtyard by the kitchen window or playing with our whip and tops, we kept a little box of coloured chalks and made patterns on the top so that when we got it spinning it looked really pretty and if it didn't we wiped it off with a bit of rag or down the side of our dress or rubbed it with our elbow, then got the chalks out and started again, we also needed to practice our 'two ball' up the wall, and he didn't want to do that so he was 'mardy' an all. The other thing we liked doing was 'hand-stands' - up the wall, we would tuck our dresses in our knicker legs so they didn't fall over our heads when we launched ourselves up the wall, at first we were afraid and our feet didn't reach the wall, but we helped each other by catching hold of the other one's legs and putting their feet on the wall, then we would get the giggles and our elbows would bend and we would end up in a heap squashed against it but it didn't take long for us to get the hang of it and when we asked our mam to watch, she said, 'You lot are a dab hand at that.' She always said that when we got things right, we were soon going to Stocks Meadow, just a little way down Sunderland Street, because it had a long grassy hill which was just the thing we needed to practice cartwheels as it was easier if we did them on a hill and also very good for roly-poly, you could go all the way to the bottom doing that. We loved Stocks Meadow in the summer with its daisies, kingcups, and cowslips everywhere and when the snow came it was a winter wonderland that we played in with our home-made toboggans having lots of fun sliding down or making snowballs.

In the early evening we would go to the Butter Cross with our friends and play on the steps, we played, salt, vinegar, mustard, pepper now, what you had to do was; one person was 'it' and would stand on the road, facing away from the steps, each step had a name, the top one was salt, the next vinegar, then mustard and the bottom one was pepper. Everyone else chose a step to start off with, when everybody was ready 'it' would say what step you had to jump to, now if you were on salt, and 'it' called mustard, you would have to reach mustard without standing on any other step, salt to pepper would mean you leaping from top to bottom and if you were on pepper and 'it' called salt, then you would be out as it was impossible to jump from bottom to top and it would be your turn at being 'it'. There was an awful lot of noise when we were playing this, there was shouts of 'Cheat' if 'it' turned round to see what steps everyone was on to try and get someone out, there were also lots of grazed hands and knees at the end, to take home to be bathed. Our mam always knew when we were playing on the steps - we really did have a thing about steps didn't we? She told us she could hear us roaring our heads off from home, when Mam wanted us in she would stand in the courtyard and call, at the top of her voice, 'Lionel, Doreen, Joyce, Enid.' Her voice getting louder and louder with each name, and by the time she got to Enid the 'id' would be high-pitched and held as long as possible, we would hear her and go quiet hoping she would leave us for another ten minutes or so, you see we knew she couldn't come and get us because of her bad leg, but then she would be off again and we knew we had better go home. As we got under the arch, Mam would be standing by the open door with her slipper in her hand waving it at us, saying 'Get in now and I won't use this,' then - waving the slipper again 'but I will if I have to tell you once more.' So we had to run the gauntlet, one at a time we would set off to run past her, then stop as the slipper was raised, then we would all be laughing, Mam would have to steady herself by putting her hand on the wall, we would see our chance and dart through the door, she often caught the top of our head as she waved the slipper about in the air, then would walk in behind us, pleased with herself for rounding us up.

Doreen, Enid and me slept in the little room the one with the bibles in. Through the window we could see into the library that had no books in it. They used to hold dance nights, which Kath, Millie and Margaret nearly always went to - we would look through the window to see them, we could even hear the music too. They really loved dancing; they did the Military Two Step, which was an easy one for us to spot them in because everyone danced in lines, the old-fashioned Waltz, which is my all-time favourite, the Fox-trot, Quick Step, you had to move your feet very fast to do that one, everyone seemed to laugh and enjoy it, they even did the Tango, that looked very hard to do but they knew them all and never got out of step, we would shout and point whenever we caught sight of them and wished we were more grown-up so that we could dance too.

They did teach us to dance; we would move things around in the living room, then holding hands and singing as we moved our feet in time with theirs. They also taught us to knit and embroider. Kath had a manicure set in a big box with velvet inside and little loops to keep everything in its place. There were nail files, scissors, things to push your cuticles down so that you had a nice half moon at the bottom of each nail, buffers with mother-of-pearl handles and pig-skin pads to make your nails shine, she told us, if we did this we would never need to put nail varnish on our nails, our Kath didn't like girls with nail varnish on. She kept it on her dressing table and never minded us borrowing it as long as we asked first.

It didn't take our Lionel long to put the out houses to use, that was after Dad had chosen the one attached to the house which he said would be our coal house and the smaller one next to it Dad had already made it home for Archie and the hens who were all bantams that had moved up with us from Sunderland Street, Archie was horrid to us, when Mam asked us to collect the eggs Archie flew at us every time trying to peck our legs, he looked beautiful with all the bright colours on his feathers but he was a bird with an attitude, he used to frighten the living daylights out of us, I think we ended up having him for dinner but when our dad told us it was Archie on the table we couldn't eat him. Dad had a chopping block and a chopper in the coal house - that's probably where Archie met his doom - when it wasn't being used Dad would drive it into the block and we were told never to take it out, he used to buy logs from Sticky Elliott, who went round the village selling logs and bags of sticks an all. I suppose we had a coal house when we were in Sunderland Street but since it was of no interest to us we didn't bother to find out - one thing that was just dawning on us, was that the pit Dad worked at was nothing like the one that Walter nearly fell into, but a coal mine. This is why he needed a coal house because Dad had a ton of coal delivered every month to our home. One day when we came home from school, we could hardly see up the yard for all this coal, I had never seen so much coal before, although it must have been arriving every month at The Gas House, I can't imagine how I missed it. As we grew older Dad would ask us to get the coal in - I don't mean a bucket full to put by the fire, that was easy, I mean a whole ton, he would tell us he had put sixpence on the copper in the wash house for one of us and if anyone else were to help they would get one too. Cyril and Lionel used to do it most of the time and we would do a bit in the hope of getting sixpence off our dad, which he usually made us share, but he did give us all his sweet coupons - everything was still on ration even food and clothes, it seemed you had to have coupons for everything. When all our sweet coupons had gone, he pretended that we had had all his too, but then he would produce them and off we would go to Mr Snell's sweet shop on the corner and buy sticks of liquorice or arrowroot, aniseed balls or gob stoppers. Mr Snell sold everything and since we didn't need to cross a road to get there - even if we had no money we still looked in his window. I went to look one day and he had just done his Christmas display and it looked lovely with lots of cotton wool for snow and silver tinsel weaving in and out of jigsaw puzzles and kaleidoscopes, cowboy hats and gun holsters, pretty wooden pencil boxes, pen and pencil sets, fairy wands and pretty wings and all kinds of books - puzzles, colouring, cut-out ones and right in the middle a big square reading/picture book called 'The Red Spotted Handkerchief' and just by looking I fell in love with it and I really wanted to have it. When I went home I mentioned it to me mam and asked if I could have it for Christmas and she said 'We'll see' oh she always said that - every day I looked through Mr Snell's window to see if it was still there, I asked Mam if I could ask him to put it by for me but she said 'No you must wait and see.' Day after day I looked in the window then one day it was gone, so that was that, but on Christmas Day morning it was all wrapped up at the bottom of the bed and I said under my breath - 'Thank you Mam.'

Lionel was looking for things to do in the out houses and soon came up with the idea of keeping rabbits, so with his friend Richard, who lived just across the road they asked Mam if it would be alright to use the out house with all the windows and the long bench - Mam said they could just as long as they looked after them properly. When they brought them home we went to have a look, they were beautiful and Doreen fell in love with them right away and was always in there talking to them, giving them tit bits, grooming and even cleaning out the hutches if she was asked, and they did ask. Lionel and Richard said they were Chinchilla and the black and white ones were English and they had to be brushed every day, they liked dandelion leaves to eat and straw to sleep on. What they didn't do was to tell Mam that they were buck and doe rabbits.

Before you could say 'Jack Robinson' Lionel and Richard were building nesting boxes in the long bit - the bit that Lionel called the slaughter house as it was dark in there. They bought more rabbits to breed from and before long they were entering them in shows and bringing home rosettes. It was nice when the babies were born, but they wouldn't let us peep too soon as Lionel said if we did the mother would kill them, that did happen once or twice even though we hadn't peeped.

The rabbits were in hutches all along the bench, nesting boxes in the long bit and babies at different stages of growth. They sold some every so often to help keep the numbers down, but still with so many rabbits that needed grooming and feeding, we got roped in to looking for dandelion leaves. Lionel would give us a sack and send us off to look for some in the fields and lanes, we couldn't get into the orchard or we might have found some in there, now sometimes we didn't want to go, especially if it was raining or cold, but he had an ally - in Doreen - she would do anything if there was an animal involved, she didn't even mind the white mice - we always went, 'reluctantly'. This went on for quite a while before they decided not to breed any more and sell the ones they didn't put into shows - shortly after that, they sold all they had left, along with the hutches, until the only thing left in the out house were the bicycles, Dad's, Millie's, with a basket on the front and Cyril's racer, he sometimes gave us a ride on the cross bar, if he saw us around Lindrick or down Water Lane.

I think it was Richard's idea to get some homing pigeons, these were going to be kept in one of the stables opposite the orchard door, they put perches along the back wall for them to roost, and made everything ready for them. They brought them home in a proper pigeon basket along with a bag of grain for them to eat. They didn't let them out for a few days, when they did it was just to let them get their bearings, as they disappeared over the top of the big barn. I thought they would just fly away, how could they possibly know where they lived, but before long one or two were sitting on top of the barn. Lionel and Richard had a handful of grain and threw some on to the ground, before long they all returned and were eating the grain, gradually making their way into the stable for the night. I can tell you that, that impressed me no end. Now they were getting fed-up with the pigeons and we got the job of coaxing them home to roost, holding grain and sprinkling it around, while all the time coo-cooing to encourage them in, while 'they' were cooking up something else to do.

They set about making a swing in the big barn and it ended up as a long thick rope thrown over a high beam - they must have used the stable next door to climb into the manger then into the loft to have thrown the rope over the beam. To have a go on it you had to lay a piece of wood across the rope then sit on it quickly before it fell off - you had to be pushed 'cos if you tried to work it up like you could on the swings in the football field the wood would slip and pinch your bum. Now I loved swings and the higher I went the better I liked it and I couldn't wait to get on this one. Lionel and Richard tried it out first then our Doreen, Enid and me had a go and we liked it, so now we were swinging away one after the other and in-between amusing ourselves in the yard. When it was my turn again Lionel and Richard started to push me - one from the back and - one from the front and I was going to go a bit higher this time. It was a good swing, swinging right out to the barn doors and back, almost touching the wall, I felt like I was on a trapeze it was great, then they were pushing me too hard and I asked them to stop before I fell off but they just called me 'scardy cat' and carried on so, I said 'That's it then, I'll tell Mam when I do get off, then you'll be sorry.' All of a sudden the wood slipped and I fell off just as I was swinging back and almost knocked myself out crashing up against the back wall. The next thing I knew, I was crying and wanted to go to me mam, but they wouldn't let me get up until I stopped crying and promised not to tell what had happened, so I stopped crying and made my promise, I suppose even if I had told me mam or dad they would probably have said 'Wait till I get hold of them, I'll knock their blocks off.' They always said that when we told tales on each other - I loved playing with them but at times like this I thought they were horrid.

Richard had a border collie called Jack - guess who liked him best? - It was decided that we would go camping as Richard had a tent an all, so we sent our Enid off to ask our mam and to our surprise she said we could, even though we told her we would be sleeping in the tent all night, she still said it would be alright, we also told her not to worry as Jack would protect us. She happily gave us some food and drink and off we all went to find a spot not too far from home - as it was already the middle of the afternoon. We went through the fields and settled for a spot near a stream, to pitch the tent - you always pitched a tent near water we were told, by 'them' and we could wash the dishes later in the stream and our hands and faces in the morning, uh, they thought they knew everything. A few hours later we had lit a fire, opened a tin of beans and put them in a pan on the fire, before long we had eaten everything Mam had packed for us and Jack had eaten all his food an all, it was getting a little bit darker and as if that wasn't enough some cows had appeared from nowhere and were nosing around us getting closer and closer. Well, that was it, we jumped up, put the fire out, shooing the cows away but making them even nosier, grabbing all our things we threw them over the fence then threw ourselves over after them. When we got home Mam was not surprised, she just smiled knowingly and told us to get ready for bed, no wonder she let us go, she just knew we wouldn't' stay out all night, she knew us 'inside out and backwards' that's for sure.

CHAPTER SEVENTEEN

WATER LANE

Water Lane begins opposite Lindrick Cottage where we were all born; it's a very long lane with water flowing along the left-hand side and a high grassy bank with a narrow footpath along the top at the other, the lane itself, just a rough cart track - now sometimes we would see the farmer bringing the cows up for milking and we soon scrambled up the bank onto the path to get out of their way only to find one or two cows already up there and getting nearer to us, but the farmer always managed to coax them down just in time but we had to look out for cow pats after they had gone by - phew cows are great big beasts especially close up.

In the long summer holidays, it always seemed warm and sunny; we would spend our time down Water Lane. Our mam would make us jam sandwiches, slice up some of her lovely home-made caraway seed cake and put them in separate bags so that we carried our own and didn't fight over who would carry the lot, we had a bottle of pop or sometimes water, we had to carry these bottles home again as we got money back on them - something we did not like doing and last of all a towel and off we would go. We loved playing around Lindrick and always went by way of the two wooden bridges. The stream that ran between the meadow and the lane was where the older boys used to gather, daring each other to jump over the stream. They had different jumps, some wider than others, they would go across the lane so they could get a good run at it, if someone did a wide jump for the first time everyone would cheer, but sometimes they fell in and always ended up with wet feet, we had to be careful when we passed them 'cos if one of them had set off running across the lane to jump they would knock us flying.

As we got into Water Lane we would sometimes stop, to take our sandals off, I liked my sandals they were brown leather on the top with little flower petals cut out, a strap and buckle to hold them on and crepe soles, they were nice and comfy - even if you took your ankle socks off they were comfy, as soon as they were too shabby for school we would wear them for play and have a new pair for school. We would sit on the bank and dabble our feet in the water for a while before carrying on down to the paddling pool, that's what we called it as there was no bank to keep the water back and so it spilled out on to the lane making it very shallow and at this point, across the water was a grassy bit with a five-barred gate to the field behind. We would always find some of our friends here, either by the gate or on the high bank near the path on the opposite side and while we were catching up on what was going on, we placed our lunch on the bank, off came the sandals again and with our dresses tucked into our knicker legs we would soon be paddling about looking for sticklebacks, we didn't catch them we just liked finding them, we would often see a shoal of them, tiny weenie things darting this way and that in unison, they were fascinating to watch. It was mostly us girls that played here, the boys would go a little further down and round the bend in the lane to the sheep dip, there was a wall at either side of the stream starting level with the lane and going deep down into the water, when the farmer used it to dip his sheep he had special boards which would slot into place at each end of the walls, putting the one furthest down stream in first, he waited for the water level to rise, when it was level with the lane he slotted the second board into place. There were two farm gates that crossed over the lane, leaving a narrow path for people to walk by, these would be closed one at a time, the sheep would be let in and the second gate closed, the farm hands drove a few sheep at a time into the water, dunking them with a long pole, then dragging them out, opening the gate, letting them out, then starting all over again until all the sheep were done. Phew, I bet the men were tired after that day's work, good job sheep didn't need a bath every week. Needless to say the farmer always took his wooden boards away with him and so leaving the water to flow at its own level, the boys that played there always managed to find some wood to make the water deep enough for them to jump in or swim.

In the meantime, back at the paddling pool we would be busy putting stepping stones across the stream to the grassy bit and collecting rocks to build a dam of our own so that we had enough water to come up to our knees, the boys would soon know what we were up to when their water level went down, they wasted no time in getting to us and knocking our dam down, we always tried to stop them but they always won. It didn't matter; we would build it again tomorrow, all being well. We would finish what was left of our lunch, drink our pop, dry our feet, sandals on and we were ready for home.

Sometimes if we were not feeling too tired we would go the long way home and that would mean going past the sheep dip and all the way to the bottom of Water Lane and where the lane turned sharply right there was a stile that we climbed over into a field that led us into Stocks Meadow. What we always seemed to forget was the steep hill we had to climb to get into Sunderland Street, then we would argue as to whose idea it was to come this way in the first place - now we had to walk all the way up to the Butter Cross, we never learned, just did it the same way time after time.

The Ashmore twins opened a dance school after the war. My friend Shirley attended and so did some of our other friends and they were enjoying it, Doreen and I wanted to join, our Enid wasn't fussed, so we asked Mam about it and she said 'Yes, anything to keep you out of mischief.' The class was held on a Friday evening in the parish room. The first thing we were taught was, tap dancing, starting with, shuffle step, then shuffle hop step, we didn't have proper tap shoes to begin with, but it wasn't long before Mr Timpson, the cobbler was busy fitting tap plates to, 'past their best' school shoes. As we learned more steps, Mrs Ashmore, the twin's mother played the piano, the idea being to get some rhythm into our movements, I can tell you the noise was deafening, but we did get better. Quite a lot of children left after the first few weeks, which made the class size more manageable, and there was a bit more routine. The twins introduced acrobatics, and our Doreen liked that better than tap. I liked it, but not better than tap. Shirley used to come to our house and we practised together.

It wasn't long before the Ashmores started a ballet class, this was on Monday evenings, because they couldn't' book the parish room for Mondays it was held in a hall in Westgate, almost opposite Auntie Annie's shiny, red brick house. I really wanted to attend this class especially as Shirley told me she was going, so I was pestering Mam to let me go but she couldn't afford it and said, if she let me go then Doreen would want to go as well, so we had to sort it out between ourselves. I knew that Doreen was down Water Lane with her friends, I didn't waste a minute, I ran out of the door, along Castlegate, round the Mill Dam, not even bothering with the two wooden bridges, just carried on racing round the lane and only when I got to Water Lane did I slow down and started to think what I was going to say to our Doreen, for all I knew she could be thinking of asking Mam if she could go to the ballet class, but somehow, I didn't think so. I was walking quite slowly by the time I got to the paddling pool, praying that she would let me go. Doreen was sitting on the grassy bank, talking and laughing with her friends, we said hello and I plonked down beside her, she looked at me and said 'What's up with you?' I blurted everything out in one breath - 'I want to go to the ballet class and Mam can't afford for both of us, so is it alright if you stop and I carry on?' she said 'Oh goo on then.' Jumping up and shouting 'Oh thanks Doreen.' I was racing back home to tell me mam.

Everyone at the school was going to have a class dress so this was more money that me mam had to find for me, Mrs Ashmore was in charge, she bought the material, and we had to go, a few at a time to be measured at their home which was in Sunderland Street, then go back for fitting, they were brown with a gold satin lining, a plain bodice with a short, flared skirt, the finishing touch was a row of sequins round the neckline and on the hem of the skirt. The class looked much better with everyone dressed the same. Over the months we were taught various tap routines plus Scottish reels, The Sailor's Hornpipe, Dutch clog dances, my dancing was developing well. I did some acrobatics; we practised the splits, cartwheels and overs, when doing this we had to make sure we landed in a 'neat' crab position, sometimes throwing our legs back to stand up, instead of raising our arms.

The Monday ballet class was much quieter than Fridays. We did a lot of bar work, learning all the foot and arm positions, stretching our bodies this way and that to loosen our limbs. It was much harder work; the twins would keep us at it no matter how tired we were. Me and Shirley went for a private ballet lesson every week to their home, we had to keep an exercise book, writing down names of positions and steps, so what with the cost of that and the extra money needed for ballet shoes and stuff, plus I was now taking exams and needed entry fees I thought me mam would say she couldn't afford it anymore - but she never did.

In the summer time, garden fetes were held in the village, I remember one in particular at Westgarth House, a big house just by Rowland Bridge, with a stream running through the beautiful gardens. There were stalls with hoop-la, lucky dip, coconut shy, white elephant stalls, this was a mish-mash of things from books and toys to china and glass, the vicar always attended and the Miss Ashmores' Dance School performed. We also did a pantomime in the library one Christmas, it was Cinderella and my friend Shirley was Buttons - she was a very good one an all, we all had a treat at the end as we were allowed to go into the audience to see the twins dance a ballet, oh, if only I could dance like that - well I can dream can't I?

Our Lionel in the meantime had a drum kit, Richard had a guitar and Gordon had an old washboard and some thimbles on his fingers which he would rub up and down the washboard making one heck of a racket, he also had a tea chest that he stood upside-down and made a hole in the top just big enough for a stick to go through then he tied a piece of string to the top and attached the other end to the side of the tea chest. When he wasn't on his washboard he would have one foot up on the tea chest plucking away at the string - they said they were a Skiffle group - now our mam wasn't impressed and she wouldn't let them play anywhere within ear shot and packed them off to the attic telling them to make a 'din' up there, so they did, they put posters all over the walls and would often go up there to practice, we would sneak up and listen then burst in and annoy them, I don't think they ever played anything properly but I'm sure they had lots of fun trying.

CHAPTER EIGHTEEN

PETS

One day we got home from school to find a dog curled up underneath the table, Dad had a big smile on his face, while Mam didn't look happy at all because father had brought another dog home, Doreen went into her usual routine - diving under the table, fussing and talking to the dog. He was a border collie cross, not a young pup, more like a teenager. We all loved him, we couldn't help it he was so loveable, we named him Bruce, which really suited him, he never needed a lead, he followed us everywhere, he didn't like being left behind. If we didn't want him with us we asked Mam to keep him in, but it was the same old story, someone would soon be coming through the door and he would be out after us. Whenever we did this we would be looking back to see if he was following, he was so cute he bobbed into doorways allowing us to get far away from home as to not be bothered to take him back. He was so clever, he seemed to know what we would do, but we really didn't mind and would call him to join us. He loved coming down Water Lane and would get into the water as soon as possible, half swimming, half walking, all the way to the paddling pool - he liked us to splash him, and would jump up to try and catch the water with his mouth.

At about this time, the churchyard was almost full and they were preparing a cemetery in the field opposite the church gates, they had sheep in the field to keep the grass down, there was a stone wall along the front, with the field going up hill, so making the wall on that side very low, the lane was much lower than the field making the wall on this side very high. Bruce must have got out of the house and, looking for us made his way round to the church and seeing the sheep in the field which had not had sheep in before, he went in and rounded them up, Bruce frightened them and two of them jumped over the low wall and they were unprepared for the drop on the other side - hurting themselves. The farmer went mad when someone told him and went straight to the field to see what had happened - someone had told him that it was Bruce and he got the bobby to come round to see Mam - when we got home Mam asked if Bruce was with us, we said 'No, why?' When she told us we defended him saying he would not do a thing like that, he wouldn't hurt anything. Mam said 'He is a sheep dog and that's what sheep dogs do.' The bobby said he had killed one and if that is so he will go on to kill again - Mam must see to it that he didn't. When Cyril came home Mam told him to take Bruce to the farmer and ask him to shoot Bruce. Cyril went off with Bruce on a piece of rope, he never did have a lead, we cried and cried, and were inconsolable - we really couldn't believe he had to be shot - no one seemed to be giving him the benefit of the doubt. It was some time later when Cyril came home with Bruce trotting along beside him, he told our mam that the farmer didn't have a licence to shoot dogs, he could only shoot rabbits. We breathed a sigh of relief, surely this would be the end of it. But Mam was still worried that he would now be blamed for anything that went wrong, and asked Cyril to take him into Doncaster Market. Cyril went into Doncaster every Saturday to watch wrestling and he knew there was a pet stall at the market and the man may well buy Bruce - this he did and came home with ten shillings. The following week Cyril came home from Doncaster and told Mam Bruce hadn't been sold yet, we pleaded with Mam to get him back for us - she gave in - Cyril took the ten shillings to fetch him home the following Saturday. Cyril came back from Doncaster without him saying the man wanted two pounds for him which he didn't have. Our hearts sank, then Mam gave Cyril the money to go straight back to Doncaster and get him - he caught the next bus and went straight to the market, but, Cyril was too late - Bruce had been sold and our only consolation was that at least he hadn't been shot.

We were playing in the yard one day when our Lionel turned at full speed into the arch, running up to us hardly able to stop he was out of breath and very excited and when he was excited he had trouble getting his words out, Mam said he had a stammer, and we must give him time, often we would run into the house to tell Mam something and we would finish Lionel's sentences for him, then our mam would tell us off and make us listen patiently to him no matter how long he took.

Well this day he was taking a long time to get his words out and because we didn't know what he wanted to tell us we had to listen patiently. We couldn't believe it, he knew a man who had a goat and wanted to give it away. Now we were as excited as our Lionel, jumping about telling him to go and get it before he gave it to someone else, then we thought we should ask Mam and it didn't take long to decide our Enid should ask, we always sent our Enid when we wanted anything, she was the baby you see and we told her she was the only one who got her own way, she would argue with that saying it wasn't true and it was about time somebody else asked. We promised this would be the last time and off she went to see Mam while we were organising where it would sleep and settled on the little stable tucked in the corner, facing the concrete square. Our Enid was walking down the yard and the look on her face told us Mam had said no, so we had a re-think and decided that as long as Mam didn't see us bring it home she would never know as she didn't come this far down the yard. Lionel with his friend went to get the goat. We were on pins and needles waiting for them to come back, going on to the front to look for them so we could warn them where Mam was before bringing it up the yard. We waited ages and then we saw them turn the corner at Snell's sweet shop with this beautiful, full-grown, white goat on the end of a long rope. They pulled in the rope before coming through the arch. We stood by the kitchen window and waved them on when it was all clear, they bobbed their heads down holding the goat as close to them as possible and ran under the window. At last, it was in the yard and round the corner out of sight. Once again our Doreen was in her element, stroking it, looking into its eyes and talking to it, we couldn't get her away. We went to get some grass for it to eat, at the same time realising we would have to do this every day and that would take up all our play time. Lionel came up with a bright idea - the goat could go in the orchard - he would get an iron stake strong enough to hold fast in the ground and to hold the goat safe on a long rope, she could be put in the orchard before school and at night she could sleep in the stable, now that was the best idea he had for a long time. When our Lionel opened the orchard door he came face to face with nettles and thistles he couldn't even take a step in, so he got a big stick to beat them down, banged the stake in the ground and tied the goat to it. She was munching away, her little tail going ten to the dozen, she was really happy. When we went with Lionel to put her in the stable after school, we opened the orchard door, praying she would still be there. Oh she was there alright and she had eaten everything that her rope allowed her to get at and for the first time we could actually walk through the door. When she saw us she leapt about and when Doreen tapped her own shoulders the goat stood up on her hind legs and put her front hoofs all the way up to our Doreen's shoulders - they were face to face with each other and we were laughing at them. Every day Lionel would move the stake further in so she had fresh, juicy nettles to munch. We soon found out what you couldn't do was, turn your back on her or she would butt your bum, sometimes so hard she would knock you over and that hurt, but our Doreen didn't care what she did, and if me and our Enid got mad at her we would get a telling off from our Doreen who would say 'She's only a goat, what do you expect?'

Once when we put her in the stable we decided to milk her, well she was a nanny goat and she had udders like the cows at Rawson's Farm and they were milked every day, so maybe she would be pleased that we had thought of it, we got a can and our Lionel went first, she stood quite still to begin with but soon kicked up her back legs making Lionel jump out of the way as the can went flying across the stable, not a drop of milk to be seen, our Doreen picking up the can saying 'You daft bugger, you didn't do it properly.' She prepared to have a go herself and calmed the goat down, then started, well she seemed to be doing it the way we had seen the farm hand do it at Rawson's Farm and the goat was standing still for her, but she wasn't getting any milk so she gave up and we decided not to try again. I'm sure I saw a quizzical look on the goat's face as we bedded her down and then left.

She was clearing the orchard at a rate of knots and Lionel was moving the iron stake every day and we could now see the whole orchard, it was enclosed by a low grey stone wall and had eight or nine pear trees dotted around and if she was staked close to a tree she munched away at the leaves and fruit, but we didn't mind that - we could hardly let our mam know we had found pear trees.

All good things must come to an end and they did the day our mam got suspicious and found the goat while we were at school. When we came home for tea we got a good telling off for going behind her back and she was as mad as anything with us saying 'Wait till your father comes home, he can deal with you lot.' - She wouldn't let us out, we pleaded with her, saying that at least the goat had cleared the orchard and the pears on the trees were nice to eat and if we couldn't keep the goat all the nettles would come back and anyway we liked playing there now and what's more it didn't seem fair either.

Our dad didn't tell us off too much, he came down the yard, had a look at the goat who was still in the orchard, then checked the stable, we began to think he would let us keep it, but it all came down the to fact that we had gone behind Mam's back and that would never do. So the goat had to go. We argued and made a fuss but it made no difference.

Lionel went to see this man at Tickhill Station which was up Northgate on the Doncaster Road, a long walk out of Tickhill. No trains went through the station as the line hadn't been used for years but this man looked after the station and kept goats on the embankment to keep things tidy, he told Lionel he would be pleased to have another goat, so with a lot of tears, especially from Doreen, Lionel set off with the goat up Northgate to hand her over.

CHAPTER NINETEEN

WINTER'S EVENING

Winter evenings were special. We would often gather round the table and play cards, we had a tin full of pennies that were shared out between us - our favourite game was Pontoon - we played that for hours on end, if our Cyril was home he would play too, he was a bad loser and always ended up throwing his cards down, calling us cheats and storming out, I don't know why 'cos we didn't keep our winnings, they went back in the box for next time, we used to giggle and Mam would shush us, trying to keep the peace. Sometimes we would do a jigsaw while Mam played Patience, a card game you played alone, another card game we liked was Snap we squabbled a lot over which one of us said 'Snap!' first. Our Lionel had a big skittle board made of wood we played with it on the hearth rug but we would get excited and noisy after a while and would have to put it away, but Mam didn't mind us playing with it in the square hall on rainy days.

Mam usually had a clipped rug on the go, she used to buy hessian, you could buy it with a pattern printed on or just plain and mark a pattern on it yourself, then you needed to buy bags of clips in the colours you wanted to use, these were strips of material about finger lengths and with a special hook you pushed the length down through the hessian then back up making sure that the two ends were the same length, the closer together you did this the thicker the rugs would be when finished, sometimes we helped by sorting the colours into bags.

We had lots of these rugs around the house, the most important one being in front of the Yorkshire range, they were very warm and you could wiggle your toes in them until they almost disappeared and sit on them without getting a cold bum.

Sometimes in the early evening when it was too cold to play outside with our friends we used to ask our mam if we could come in and play, she mostly said yes and we would go upstairs to our bedroom, we loved playing Hide and Seek, as there were lots of places to hide, under the beds, behind the doors, dark corners like the one at the end of the narrow landing with the balustrade along, if you bobbed down in the corner there you couldn't be seen at all, a good place was under the five stairs that led to the long landing. There was two really scary places, one were the attic stairs 'cos you could close the door behind you and the other the little bedroom in the storage bit where the big bibles were, sometimes I would hide in one or the other but if I wasn't found quick enough I'd give myself up - well I wasn't the only one, our Enid got frightened an all.

Another thing that frightened us all were the bats that flew through the arch, they always started at around dusk, flying this way and that in the big yard then swooping through the arch, our friends told us that if they got tangled in our hair it would all have to be cut off, can you imagine that? Well, my imagination was working overtime I can tell you and my knees used to knock every time I had to go through, not on my own though, we usually went through together, putting our cardies or coats over our heads and linking arms before making a dash for it.

When it was near bed time Mam would tell us to get ready for bed and take the bed warmers up - these being the oven shelves - she always wrapped them up for us in old flannelette sheets that she kept for this purpose - we put them into our beds, always pushing them half way down, then when we went up later we pushed them down to the bottom and we were as snug as a bug in a rug. When we were in our long wincyette night-gowns and Lionel had his pyjamas on, we went back down for our warm drink, if we were hungry we made toast, sitting on the hearth rug, sticking the long toasting fork through the bars of the fireguard, unless we had nipped to the chippy earlier for a bag of crispy bits. Our Lionel had a radiogram and records of Johnny Ray, Frankie Lane, Guy Mitchell, Doris Day and The Beverley Sisters, some evenings when we were all ready for bed, we played them and put on a show, dancing and singing to every record, our Doreen, Enid and me used to sing 'Sisters, Sisters' a popular song of The Beverley Sisters, almost as good as them - no kidding - I did a good impression of Doris Day singing 'You Can't Get A Man With A Gun' and made everybody laugh, once I got carried away and I kicked my leg high, forgetting my long, narrow wincyette night-gown and falling flat on my back making everyone laugh even louder until Mam would say, 'Stop now, you are making yourselves giddy.'

When the evenings were dark and we were playing happily we would never go to bed on our own or leave the living room for that matter, without one or the other of us going along too, you see although we had electricity, the light switch was never in the right place, for instance, if Mam wanted something from the front room, we needed to go to the other end of the red, tiled hall in the dark to switch the light on, get whatever it was Mam wanted from the room, switch the light off and come back along the hall in the dark, but even worse than that, to go to bed we could switch the light on at the foot of the stairs, run all the way up and put the light on in the bedroom, then run all the way back down to switch the light off again, running back up in the half dark - was there any wonder that we went around in twos or better still threes?

Once we stayed up later than usual and Uncle Jim came home from the pub, we liked our Uncle Jim a lot - on this particular evening he had had one too many and plonked himself in the chair to take his shoes off but couldn't find his laces, we were stifling our giggles, holding our mouths so he couldn't see us, he was taking ages, sitting up in-between tries, to gather himself together before trying again, after that we used to ask Mam if we could stay up until he came home and watch him again, but she never let us. Our dad used to miss all this, as he needed to go to bed early so he would be fresh for work the following day, you see he went to work very early in the morning.

Princess Elizabeth is getting married and people who had a television set would be able to see it. Mam said that Mrs Brown had just bought one and what's more we were invited to her home to see the wedding, we didn't know what to expect. When the day came Mam made sure our clothes were clean and tidy and our hair brushed then looking at us saying 'You'll do,' sent us off with instructions to be good and not to mess about and show her up or we would get a thick ear.

Mrs Brown's front room was very small, or maybe it looked that way because we were all in it, what intrigued us was the little box with knobs and things - a bit like Dad's wireless - sitting on a small table in the corner by the fireplace. Mrs Brown said it would be better for us to sit on the hearth rug leaving the chairs for the grown-ups, so we plonked down sitting cross-legged. At last the television was switched on, it whistled and crackled before the picture was clear, it was very small and I wondered how we would be able to see more than one face at a time let alone a whole wedding, but what a treat it turned out to be, seeing our Princess again, well we had seen her before don't forget. It started by showing the golden coach taking the princess to Westminster Abbey, a beautiful building and it made me wonder if ever Coventry Cathedral used to look like this. When we visited Mollie and her family in Coventry after the war - even our mam stopped getting on with things to come with us. We were taken around to see houses and shops that had been bombed - thank goodness Mollie and the children had been safe with us when all this happened. Our Doreen didn't come out every day with us as she had a bad earache but she did come on the day we went to see the cathedral which was in ruins, there was part of the front still standing and it seemed that all the rubble had been moved aside to show the isle leading the way to the alter, lots of people were walking up and down the aisle looking very sad - if the cathedral had been as beautiful as Westminster Abbey then there was little wonder at their sadness. Waiting outside the abbey were lots and lots of bridesmaids, little ones and big ones and when the golden coach stopped the Princess stepped down, her wedding dress, the like of which had never been seen before took our breath away. Inside the abbey we watched the Princess as she walked down the isle with her father the King beside her and all her bridesmaids following, oh, I had never seen anything so beautiful in all my life, the trumpets were sounding as the Princess married her Prince, the King and Queen were smiling and happy for them along with the hundreds and hundreds of people who were also in the abbey. All the bells were ringing out for them as they stepped into the golden coach that would take them back to Buckingham Palace. Every inch of the way people were cheering and waving flags - the way we were the day she came to Tickhill - the horse's hoofs clip-clopping along The Mall must have been making a racket but no one would hear because of all the cheering. Once the coach went through the gates of the palace all the people moved forward crowding around the gates and railings and the crush now was all the way back down The Mall, everyone waiting for them to step onto the balcony high up at the front of the palace. When they appeared and waved back at the crowd, a great cheer went up and the King and Queen came out to even more cheers. I thought it would never stop and they would never be able to leave the balcony - then it was all over. We thanked Mrs Brown and hurried home to tell Mam - and we did in great detail - Mam must have wished she had come with us instead of staying home getting on with things.

CHAPTER TWENTY

BABIES

Our Millie is pregnant. At last the bouncy, cream pram will have a baby in it instead of Walter or things being flitted from Sunderland Street to Castlegate. Everyone was busy knitting bonnets, booties and matinee coats, Millie was buying everything from night-gowns, nappies and romper suits to soap, talc and cotton wool, all these things were being put away in their bedroom - the one, on the right of the long landing. We were so excited and looking forward to seeing the new baby and since Mollie and Sid had gone home, taking the children with them, we had no one to look after or be in charge of.

Millie and Arthur's daughter arrived prematurely on 23rd October on our Millie's birthday - isn't that something - she was very, very tiny and Mam was worried about her - we were told we couldn't see her just yet. There was a lot of coming and going, even Mr Cook, the vicar climbed our stairs and went in to the bedroom, he christened the baby there and then - 'She's our Jennifer' - when we finally got to see her our mam took us all in to the bedroom together, it was a cold October day and there was a fire burning in the grate, the whole room was enveloped in a warm, baby soap and talc smell. Millie was laying in bed and Jennifer was in a drawer that Mam had taken from her chest of drawers, our mouths dropped open, she was tucked up in cotton wool and was no bigger than a little doll, her tiny hands and face fascinated us, we wanted a closer look but

Millie didn't want her to get cold, we did see her hair, which was ginger, just like her dad's except Jennifer's had little curls and Arthur's was dead straight. Our Millie said when the sun shines, she will be a little older and then we can push her outside in the pram.

Since Mam had told us not to stay too long and make Millie tired we reluctantly went downstairs, but when we went to bed at night and got up in the morning we would creep along and put our ear to Millie's bedroom door hoping to hear what was going on or better still, if someone heard us and let us in for a quick peep. We volunteered to carry warm water, cups of tea and the coal scuttle, anything, as long as we got in for a minute. As soon as Millie came down with Jennifer to spend the days in the living room we pestered her, wanting to hold the baby - she did let us - but would make sure we were sitting down, before she put her into our arms, just for a little while at first until she was sure we were capable. We tried not to fight over her in case Millie stopped us holding her, so we were very grown-up about it. We all went to church where Jennifer was christened for the second time and when the warm weather came we were allowed to rock her in the pram and push it, but only in the courtyard, if no one was keeping and eye on us out there, then we did fight over whose turn it was.

David arrived on 4th December 1947 in the same bedroom and once again we were hanging around, itching to see this little boy. At last we were allowed in, the room was cosy and gave us the same feeling as the day we first saw Jennifer, he had very straight ginger hair just like his dad, some of it sticking up, which made us giggle and want to touch it, Millie let us hold him if we sat in the chair by the fireplace. As he was much stronger than his big sister when he was born, he came down to the living room after a week or so and was christened in St Mary's Church, with us fussing around him. We rocked him in the cream pram, as we had Jennifer and once again were arguing as to whose turn it was and trying to force the other's hands off the pram handle, the pram tipped forward, our hearts turned over at the thought of David falling out - thankfully he didn't but us, expecting any minute for someone to come out of the house to see what was going on, stood in shock just quietly looking at each other, not a word between us - we behaved ourselves after that.

At this time the council had just completed lots of houses some had three bedrooms, some four and others even had five, they all had bathrooms and nice gardens, back and front. It was named Crown Road which we all thought was a good name as it followed on above King Edward Road.

It was soon after David was born that Millie, Arthur and their babies moved into the new house, Number One, Crown Road, it wasn't far from Castlegate and Millie popped in with the babies to see Mam every day and we were able to see them often, in fact we now went there every Saturday for a bath and a chance to play with the babies, plus stuff ourselves with Millie's home-made cakes. We loved going to our Millie's at every opportunity.

Our Margaret was still with us in Castlegate and Ernest in Rowland Cottage, by Rowland Bridge where the water flowed to join the Mill Dam, he had grown up there and still lived with his family, they got married in Tickhill Church in 1947, Margaret looking lovely in her white wedding dress, she had three grown-up bridesmaids, one of which was our Kath, Uncle Frank from Warsop was there to give her away. We were there, we loved going to weddings, we could dress up and dance around as much as we liked and there were always lots of cakes to eat and nobody seemed to notice just how many we were eating.

Margaret and Ernest moved into a cottage on Rawson's Farm in Sunderland Street - the one we used to get the milk from - you had to walk along a little cobbled yard that had two cottages in, Margaret and Ernest's being the second one. Our Margaret often popped in to see Mam and this is how we found out that she was going to have a baby. Colin was born at the cottage and we were on our Margaret's doorstep before she had time to change his nappy, running up the stairs two at a time, eager to see this new-born baby. He was beautiful with jet-black hair like his dad, and amazing, big, brown, calf-like eyes and once again we were all wanting to be the first to hold him. We visited their little cottage often.

Auntie Peggy is going to have a baby, both she and Uncle Harry are thrilled to bits but Mam is worrying again, this time because of Auntie Peggy's age, saying she could be in for a difficult birth. As the pregnancy went on Mam made sure that Auntie Peggy didn't do too much, getting her to rest her legs as much as possible.

No one was more relieved than Mam when Auntie Peggy had a beautiful, healthy little boy. Uncle Harry was like a dog with two tails and we were jumping about wanting to take a look at him, he was a lovely little boy was our Peter, with a cheeky face and fine, light brown hair. Mam said he was a proper little Cooper - he was fussed over and spoiled by all of us, especially his dad. Once again we were arguing as to who would hold him first.

It was soon after Peter was born that Auntie Peggy and Uncle Harry moved into a tiny cottage - one of a row of three or four in Sunderland Street almost opposite the Miss Ashmores' house - you stepped off the wide pavement to go through the front door then down the deep step into the living room, it seemed funny, like you might bump your head. I bet Uncle Jim always bumped his when he called 'cos he was ever so tall. We always bobbed our heads down just in case, we were forever in and out, playing with our Peter and hoping to catch Auntie Peggy taking hot bread out of the oven, well it wasn't easy for us now - our noses weren't keen enough to smell it from home, you see she had a neat little Yorkshire range in the living room so that's where she cooked now and it was all warm and cosy.

Auntie Peggy called to see Mam a lot when Peter was a toddler and we played with him in the courtyard, he loved playing with his wooden horse which had wheels and a handle bar which he could hold to push the horse along, he loved doing this but we liked sitting him on the horse so we could push him - this didn't please him, all he wanted to do was push it himself, so he was usually trying to get off and crying by the time we had all had a push before we let him get off. I think he got used to it in the end and just let us get on with it, he loved playing with us, really he did and we didn't always play with the horse - he was a cheeky little monkey always out for fun.

CHAPTER TWENTY-ONE

SENIOR SCHOOL

The only schools in Tickhill were the infant school house and the junior school, so when we were eleven years old we travelled by coach to Maltby, a small town a few miles outside Tickhill that had a mixed grammar, a girls senior and a boys senior. Two coaches, one for boys, one for girls came every school day, pulling up and waiting outside our house, very handy for us and our friends, especially if it was cold, they would call for us and come in to the warm living room to wait, my friends Shirley and Audrey used to call for me. It was a pleasant journey along a country road; the only thing we passed that I didn't like was an Ordnance factory. Uncle Harry worked there during the war so did our Kath for a short time and for a while she was in the land army, it looked scary with a high, wire fence and spiky barbed wire along the top. The coaches travelled along the main road passing the few shops that made up the town centre, turning right and going up a steep hill - the gates of the grammar school came first, a little further along were the gates to the girls senior, with the boys still higher up the hill.

I had never seen such a big school before, there were classrooms and corridors everywhere, it's a wonder I didn't get lost, the hall was enormous there was a platform with a table and a piano on it; this is where we had assembly every morning. The nice thing was, we had a different teacher for each subject, so after every lesson we moved to a different classroom, there was a science lab with Bunsen burners and other weird things that I never got to grips with, there was a special classroom for needlework which had sewing machines in it - I had never used one, all the sewing I had done so far was what Mam taught all of us, tacking before hemming and making sure it was done neatly, so I was looking forward to trying out the sewing machine. It was some time later that our class used them to make our own summer school dress, which was blue check cotton. Mam was pleased with mine and said, she couldn't have made it any better herself. There was a cookery class with ovens that didn't need coal. Doreen loved doing cookery, everything she did turned out good, her best things were cakes and she made lovely coconut macaroons. Whatever she made she would take home for Mam to taste, me and our Enid liked tasting them as well. My baking was never as good as Doreen's, it was either over-done or misshapen - in other words a bit of a mess - I usually shared it out on the coach going home, I never took mine home for me mam to see, she would have said, 'You've made a right pig's ear out of that my girl.'

The playgrounds were big and one had a netball court, I had never played the game before but I soon got to like it and got into the school team, my position help shooter, meant I could move around the whole pitch and get into the semi-circle to shoot the ball at the high basket hoping to score a goal, I was quite good at that. If it was raining or too cold for netball we stayed in the big hall and practised on the apparatus.

At lunch times we would go out of school, down the hill to the tuck shop which was just across the main road and down into the low road, you could get there by walking a little way down once you had crossed the main road - or there was another way down a flight of stone steps which had an iron bar down the centre from top to bottom - this was always worth holding on to - half way down the steps you could take a rest on a large stone platform before making your way to the bottom, much too dangerous to play salt, vinegar, mustard, pepper, we would keep that for the Butter Cross. Which ever way you chose you would still have to line up outside the tuck shop and wait your turn. Just behind the shop were 'The Crags' a large area of grassland with huge chunks of rocks cropping up everywhere, lots of us played here in the lunch break. There was an open-air swimming pool out on The Crags and in the summer the class would be taken there for swimming lessons, the water was absolutely freezing, too cold to even put your toe in, not a bit like Water Lane, so is there any wonder that I am such a poor swimmer?

At last we have talked our mam into letting us grow our hair, she agreed, on condition that we wore it in plaits, especially at school as we might easily get nits if our hair was loose, so as soon as our hair was long enough, we would kneel in front of Mam's chair so she could do the plaits, tying a ribbon on the end and making a bow, I dreaded this knowing there would be knots in my hair and Mam would pull it, but I just held on to my scalp as tight as I could, I didn't dare moan otherwise Mam would threaten to have the lot cut off. Most mornings on the coach to school we took the ribbons off and shook our hair free, then on the coach home we plaited it up again. It wasn't long before we got the dreaded nits and lice, in fact, practically everyone in the school had them, uh, they were horrible, itchy things, Mam had to put special stuff on our hair - she bought a fine-tooth comb - just the job for combing out nits and found an old tea tray that was not used anymore, so armed with all this paraphernalia, we could be found kneeling in front of our mam, our heads over the tea tray while Mam combed and combed our hair to get rid of the damned things, that's what Mam called them. I thought they would never go, but eventually they did. Mam was ever vigilant and at least once a week we had our heads over the tea tray - can't be too careful Mam would say.

The autumn term was a busy one for the music teacher, planning for the carol concert at the end of term, this involved practically every girl in the school, quite a job, what with getting the singers, singing in some sort of harmony, the girls playing instruments, hitting the right notes, there was lots of practising with Christmas carols to be learned off by heart and the teacher not happy until she was sure everything was exactly right. It was all very exciting on the evening of the concert. Mam would have a fresh school uniform, clean white ankle socks and our Sunday shoes ready for us to take to school. When lessons were over we went to the cloak room to freshen up and change, one or two teachers would be on hand getting us into some sort of order before going into the main hall which by now was packed with grown-ups. It was always a great success with everyone congratulating our poor worn-out music teacher, it had been a long day for us too and we would file out of school into the dark night and get on the coach that had been waiting to take us home.

I remember one winter's evening very well. It was over the Christmas holiday - our Mam's favourite time when everyone gathered together at our house. We had a fresh Christmas tree as usual that we always helped to dress, the baubles were very old and fragile and they came out of the Christmas trimmings box year after year so we were always told to take care with them, the other thing we took from the box were old, tin candle holders with frilly edges and a clip underneath that held them on the tree and tiny red candles - just as old and never used - which we pushed into the holders. We had silver tinsel, chocolate Santas and chocolate money to hang on and a fairy on the top, Mam always bought packs of bright coloured paper strips and we would spend our evenings just before Christmas making paper chains, short ones for the tree and longer ones to go across the ceiling. The trimmings box also held two beautiful looking Victorian paper garlands with dark red roses and holly that seemed to be sitting inside the outline of pretty Christmas boxes and stretched from one end of the room to the other, there were huge paper bells and balls to hang down from the ceiling plus fresh holly and mistletoe that we tied with cotton and hung from the ceiling too, we always made sure that we knew where the mistletoe was so we could stay away from it and we always put it on a short cotton so no one could reach it or the lads would break some off and chase us especially if our Lionel brought his friends back - you know what boys are like - always wanting to kiss girls under the mistletoe - we still thought boys were silly, not half as bright as we were.

As I was saying, this particular evening was a day or so after Christmas Day, all the grown-ups were going across the road to The Red Lion. Mam had prepared all manner of food from sandwiches, pork pie and pickles to mince pies and Christmas cake, and guess what? Our Doreen, Enid and me were put in charge of Jennifer, David, Colin and Peter. All the grown-ups were carrying trays and tins of food and all in turn telling us to behave and that someone would pop back now and again to make sure we were alright but if we needed anyone to just come over and get them.

Everything started out fine, the kiddies were playing with their new toys and were playing music and all of us munching nuts and chocolates. We had a couple of visits from the grown-ups and all was well, but that didn't last the kiddies were getting fed up with their toys and we had run out of ideas on how to keep them amused. We decided to light the candles, now we had their attention and lighting a taper from the fire we soon had all the candles alight making the tree look pretty but once it was done they couldn't see the fun in just standing looking at them and soon lost interest and we were back to square one looking for something else to amuse them - all of a sudden we saw one of the candles had caught a paper chain then another and another the kiddies were frightened and so were we for that matter - we opened the living room door and the back door - half holding - half dragging the tree we managed to get it outside, all the chocolates were melting and our paper chains had disappeared and all the grown-ups had appeared and were grabbing the crying children telling us off at the same time. Thank goodness nothing else in the house was burned, phew, it was a long, long time before we were allowed to forget that winter's evening.

Tea times on Sundays were always special, our mam liked us all to be home for Sunday tea. The table with a snowy, white cloth on would soon be filled with all kinds of mouth-watering things to eat. A glass dish with thin slices of cucumber and onion rings soaked in vinegar overnight was everyone's favourite, Mam's special glass vase gently fluted around the top in pale blue, standing tall in the centre of the table with celery in looking almost like a bunch of flowers - something our mam would never pick for the table - we had a glass, oval salt dish that you could put the tip of your finger and thumb into to pinch enough salt to sprinkle over food. There were potted meat sandwiches, pork pie, salmon, plus home-made pickled red cabbage, pickled onions and cheese - talking of cheese, Mam could make curd cheese, she would keep some milk aside in the pantry until it curdled then separated it from the whey by putting the curd into a muslin cloth and tying it tightly before hanging it over a bowl and leaving it until all the whey had drained - well I just loved this cheese and would be forever in and out of the pantry, poking at the curd with my finger to see if it was ready, then I would hear Mam call from the living room 'Will you get out of there madam and leave that cheese alone.' Now when our mam called us madam or young lady we knew we were in trouble so I got out of there quick, but it didn't' stop me sneaking in again the following day trying to hurry it along in time for Sunday tea.

Everyone loved Mam's home-made fruit cake, our dad used to eat it with cheese but I liked my cheese, especially curd with bread and butter and sometimes I would have cucumber soaked in vinegar with it - yum, yum. Apart from the fruit cake there were lots of buns and tarts and what we liked best of all was tinned fruit with Carnation milk poured over it or custard, a hard choice to make which would have Mam hovering with Carnation in one hand and custard in the other telling us to hurry up or we would get neither. The big brown teapot full of freshly brewed tea went down well with us all. Uncle Frank and Auntie Hetty came over from Warsop to have tea with us sometimes, I liked it when they were at the table with us - it made it kind of special.

Our Enid had a paper round and got up very early to pick up her bag from Mr Snell's shop on the corner she put the bag on the front of her bike before setting off up Northgate to deliver the papers so by the time she got back home it was a rush for her to have breakfast and get ready for school and she did this for quite a long time. Mr Snell said she was the best paper girl he had ever had as she never let him down.

Well one day our Enid was poorly so I went instead. I nearly collapsed under the weight of the bag and I'd only carried it out of the shop and put it on the bike but now I was all set to start - every house had a garden gate that I had to remember to close behind me and a path some long, some not so long, phew, I was popping papers through doors, nipping in and out of gates and the paper bag feeling no lighter. I never thought of Northgate as being a long walk but when you have walked up and down every garden path on the way it takes you forever and knocks the stuffing out of you as well, I didn't know what time it was for all I knew the school bus could have gone by now and I had to get all the way back home. I rushed in to the shop and plonking the bag on the counter, Mr Snell said 'Everything alright Joyce?' and rushing back out, I called 'Yes, all done,' and ran home pleased with myself, I had breakfast and jumped on to the school bus which hadn't left after all.

Enid did the round as usual the following day and when she got back home she was mad at me - by all accounts I had put half the papers through the wrong letterboxes and the customers were running to and fro waving the wrong papers about trying to find theirs and not only that but they called into Mr Snell and complained to him and that made him mad. There were a lot of mad people about that day our Enid was livid because the customers didn't know it was me that delivered them and were blaming her for it, I shouted that it wasn't my fault if the papers were put in the wrong order and Enid shouting back that they weren't and that 'The papers all had the house numbers on and you should have looked at them, you silly sod.' It was all getting a bit heated, Mam calmed us down then told me to get off and apologise to Mr Snell and say sorry to our Enid for messing it up. I had a red face for a long time after with people calling things, like 'Don't let your Joyce get hold of your paper bag, Enid' - and she didn't.

CHAPTER TWENTY-TWO
HELPING OUR MAM

With Millie, Arthur, Jennifer and David now living in their own house and Margaret, Ernest and Colin in their farm cottage and a short time after, Aunt Peggy, Uncle Harry and Peter moved into a little cottage of their own, there was room to spare at home. Mam would often take in a lodger if the proprietors of The Red Lion Public House opposite were full they would send them over to Mam. One regular was Pete he delivered fresh fish and always arrived in a large refrigerated truck that he was able to drive through the arch into the big yard, everyone liked him, he called our Mam, Aunt Rose and said our house was home from home to him. We were growing up now and we had jobs to do around the house, some before we went to school and some after school. Every morning we made all the beds before going to school and ran any errands Mam needed. We did the washing-up taking turns to wash, wipe and put away, arguing whose turn it was to do what as usual. We swept and dusted everywhere and washed the bedroom floors once a week. The bare, wooden staircase and landings had to be scrubbed every week - Mam kept an eye on us when we did this job - making sure we scrubbed no more than two steps at a time. The red brick hall was also scrubbed once a week - the front room was cleaned thoroughly whether it had been used or not and the fire grate always laid ready - then the furniture had to be polished.

By now Mrs Crossland had moved into the Alms Houses and I cleaned for her every Saturday morning, taking anything with me Mam thought she would need, along with her clean laundry. It wasn't very far for me to go, just a little way along Casltegate, turning into the bridal path and just by the church wall were the Alms Houses, they were built around a pretty square garden. Mrs Crossland was usually up by the time I got there even though I was always early and I had a key with me. As you opened the front door you were in a good-sized room and at the back was a door to the scullery, so it really didn't take much cleaning, Mrs Crossland had her bed in the main room along with a table, chairs and a small chest of drawers with amongst other things a wireless on the top - she still listened to Mrs Dale's Diary, there was an armchair by the open fireplace and a few rugs here and there. I would first make her a cup of tea, if she hadn't already had one, then I would get on - taking the rugs outside for a good shake - clearing the fireplace of any cinders if it had been used and laying a fresh one. I changed her bed putting on the fresh sheets and pillow slips I had brought with me - washed the floor of the main room and the scullery - dusted and polished everything, setting the rugs in place and all the while we chatted to each other. If she needed anything from the shops I would nip and get it although it was very rare, as Mam seemed to know just what she needed and sent it along with me. I did this every week for a long time. If for some reason I couldn't do it then our Doreen or Enid would go in my place. One Saturday I went off as usual - when I reached the door it was still locked - I thought nothing of it as it had happened once or twice before when she had over-slept or gone straight off to the scullery to put the kettle on so I used my key to get in and she was still in bed. I put my bag of things on the table and walked over to the bed calling good morning, I moved the covers and realised that she was dead - I don't know how I knew that - just for a moment I panicked, then knew exactly what I must do. I didn't take my bag I just left the house quietly, locking the door behind me. I made my way onto the bridle path then I set off running as fast as my legs would carry me all the way home. I was out of breath when I reached the living room and on seeing Mam I started to cry, telling her what had happened, although Mam couldn't walk very well she came back with me - knowing just what to do, set everything in motion before we left together with Mam leaning heavily on my arm all the way home.

Mrs Crossland was buried in Tickhill Churchyard with her husband - she would be happy now.

Monday was washday. Early in the morning the fire underneath the copper had to be lit, water had to be fetched from the living room sink in buckets, until the copper was full. In the meantime back in the living room Mam was organising herself, you see our mam's bad leg wouldn't let her stand for too long, so now she got on with things sitting down - she had a chair by the sink to sit on and another with the bathtub on - this was kept in the wash house and only used on washdays now. The other thing that was kept in the wash house was the washtub on legs with a wringer on the back - the rollers were much smaller than the ones that used to be outside Auntie Annie's kitchen window - they did a good job so this was brought into the red square hall by the door, the lid on the top had a handle in the centre and attached underneath a paddle, so when you moved the handle from left to right the paddle swished the clothes around in the water. Mam didn't think much of this contraption for getting clothes clean and just used it for a cold water rinse with a bag of Dolly Blue dipped in. When the water in the copper was hot enough to use, starting with the white clothes, Mam took one item at a time dunking it in to the bathtub, and using her rubbing board she draped the item across then with the big bar of Fairy Soap rubbed up a lather and scrubbed and scrubbed up and down the board, she wrung it out with her hands then put it into the sink, this process was carried out time and time again until the sink was full. Then the clothes were taken across the courtyard to the copper where the water was now boiling and soap powder added, wooden tongs were used to put the clothes in and to take them out as they were boiling hot, they were taken back to Mam and put in the bathtub where she would inspect them rubbing away at any marks she saw before they went into the sink for a rinse and then into the washtub which contained the Dolly Blue, where they were swished around before being put through the wringer and were ready for the clothes lines, which were already zigzagging across the big yard. We hated washday if it was raining, because the clothes would have to be dried around the fire and seemed to be hanging around for ages. By the end of washday our mam was dog tired but even so everything would be tidy and back to normal with a hot meal ready for our dad when he came home from work.

On Tuesday Mam did the ironing, this was done on the big, wooden table in the living room, a blanket and sheet kept specially for ironing on she spread out over half of the table - two flat irons were on the Yorkshire range getting hot also she had a small dish of cold water that she would put her fingers in and splash water over anything that was badly creased. Everything was sorted before she started. She never ironed sheets, these were pulled as they came off the line, two of us, one taking the top end the other the bottom would gather the sheet with our fingers, then pulled the sheet as taut as possible moving our hands backwards and forwards stretching it into shape then neatly folding it, any that we found needing to be patched we would put to one side, Mam made neat patches - these sheets usually ended up on our beds but we never minded. There was always a never-ending pile of shirts and separate starched collars to be ironed and almost as many school blouses, loads of pillow and bolster slips and handkerchiefs by the dozen, these were placed one on top of the other, one pile for men's and one for lady's, this made them quicker to iron, the socks were put into pairs and checked, any with holes in were put into her sewing box to be darned, Mam had darning wool of all colours in the sewing box along with a wooden mushroom that she used for this job she pushed the mushroom into the sock stretching the hole over it, then popping her thimble over her finger she would start to darn, it was fascinating to watch her weaving the wool in and out and making tight little squares so that the sock would still be comfortable to wear, the shirts were always checked for missing buttons, Mam had a button box an all, and no matter how many shirt buttons were missing she had a never-ending supply and after a quick sort through her box, stitched them on before anyone knew they were gone. We helped with the handkerchiefs and sometimes the pillow slips but not the shirts; Mam said we would have to watch her some more before she let us try. Sometimes she let us but if it looked like we would mess it up she would say 'Out of the way you are neither use nor ornament' and we would try again another day.

Mam always did her baking mid-week, caraway seed cake, fruit cake, fairy cakes, jam and lemon curd tarts and all kinds of fruit pies, we used to go blackberry picking, we knew exactly the ones to pick then Mam would make a blackberry pie, the other thing she put them in was Yorkshire puddings - pouring the batter into the tin then sprinkling the blackberries in and when they came out of the oven she sprinkled sugar over then we poured our mam's specially made blackberry vinegar all over and they were 'yummy'. Our dad always had a big Yorkshire pudding almost every day - not a blackberry one - Mam served it up as a starter on a big dinner plate and Dad poured gravy on and put lots of salt and pepper on, if we were in we used to put our elbows on the table waiting for a taste, our dad's Yorkshire pudding always seemed to taste better than ours. We loved being in the living room when Mam was baking, the smell was delicious and she always gave us the bowl to run our finger round. One or the other of us would fetch the pastry board and rolling pin, the cake tins and the ingredients she needed from the cupboard or pantry putting them on the table for her, if she was short of anything we nipped over the road to the grocery shop. The coals on the fire had to be burning well to get the oven hot because Mam didn't like to put more coal on in the middle of baking, as it would loose heat. One day I was doing this job, I had nipped to the shop for her and everything was ready then Mam found she was short of something and asked me to go again. I must have been wanting to go and play because I moaned saying 'I have already been over and I'm not going again.' As soon as I had said it I knew I would be sorry. Mam didn't shout at me she just struggled to her feet saying she would go herself, she hadn't crossed over the road on her own for ages and I panicked saying I would go and I was sorry begging her to tell me what she wanted - we were out onto the pavement by now and I was trying to hold her arm in case she fell, I was crying trying to stop her but she pulled away from me saying 'Get in the house you little madam' so I went, shaking from head to toe waiting for her to come back. When she did I went to help her again but she shrugged me off telling me she didn't need my help anymore. I ran upstairs to my bedroom still crying, after a while she called from the bottom of the stairs for me to come down but I didn't answer, she called again then in a very angry voice said 'Right madam stay where you are and if you think you are going to your dance class you can think again because that money has been stopped.' There was a long silence, oh how I wished I had gone to the shop, I wished I had gone downstairs when she had called, I wanted to do a wee, if I didn't go down soon I would have to use the chamber pot under the bed and then I would be in more trouble for using it through the day, I had been up there for ages when I heard footsteps on the stairs I just hoped it wasn't Mam having to come up for me as I knew it was a great effort for her to climb them but it was our Kath, she had just come home and Mam had sent her to get me, she sat by me on the bed telling me to stop crying and then she would take me down, thank goodness she was going to take me I don't think I would have had the courage to go down on my own. I felt so ashamed of what I had done, Kath held my hand and walked me into the living room, Mam gave me an old-fashioned look all her anger gone she said 'Get in here young lady and sit at the table for your tea.' - What a Mam we had - come Friday I sheepishly asked if I could go to my dance class, she gave me the money, I had learned another hard lesson.

Friday was the day that the living room was cleaned thoroughly, and that means all the rugs were taken up and put on the line in the yard to be beaten. If it was a nice day left on the line to freshen up. The Yorkshire range would have a very low fire to allow it to cool down, ready for cleaning. Mam had a cleaning box especially for this job, there was 'black lead' which was in a screw topped tin, brushes that were shaped like a rocker with a handle over the top there were three or four of these, some with hard bristles and others with very soft ones, lots and lots of dusters and squares of velvet. The first job was to put the black lead on with a cloth, a small area at a time, then brush it with a hard brush, then with a soft one, until the whole range was done, then polished with a cloth until you could see your face in it, and the finishing touch was to wipe it over with the velvet square. Now all of that took a very long time and believe me you were very hot by the end of it. Apart from this the companion set had to be cleaned with Brasso, the hearth washed and the fire banked up with coal and the big fireguard put in place.

The next job was the floor had to be scrubbed. We would have a big bucket of hot water and a great big bar of Sunlight Soap, a scrubbing brush and floor cloth plus a kneeling mat. It was a very large area to scrub, we used to try and do as big a patch as we could so that we would be finished sooner, but Mam would tell us to do smaller pieces otherwise there would be tidemarks. Mam didn't like tidemarks, not on necks or floors and so it took us ages to finish but it made Mam happy and that was all that mattered. Whatever job Mam wanted us to do the first thing she would say is, 'Just put your pinafore on and do that for me,' our mam was funny, if we didn't have one on she said 'Where's your pinnie?'

By the afternoon, before Dad got home the furniture was polished, the rugs put down and everything back in place with the fire glowing, the water hot and the meal almost cooked and the tea mashed. Mam always made sure that the house was ship-shape and comfortable before our dad came home from work.

CHAPTER TWENTY-THREE

DAD

Our dad is poorly, he has TB like Kath. He gets very tired and hasn't enough energy to go to work every day, Mam begged him to give up the pit but he wouldn't hear of it - he reasoned - if he did, the delivery of coal would stop and how would we manage to keep the hungry Yorkshire range going and heating the other rooms upstairs and down.

Dad is getting too weak to even walk so Mam has got a wheelchair and often tucks Dad up with a blanket around his legs and pushes him through the arch and leaves him to sit awhile to have a chat to the folks going by, our mam says it perks him up a bit. When she brings him back into the living room he tells her who he has seen and what has been said, if he tells her something she finds hard to believe, she says the same thing she always says to Mrs Brown or Mrs Bradder when they have a chat - 'That's all my arse and Peggy Martin,' now we didn't know a Peggy Martin and what our mam's arse had to do with anything is anyone's guess. Mam had their bed brought downstairs and put in the front room, she is now nursing Dad, day and night, feeding, bathing and changing him and just being there whenever he needs her.

Around this time I was taking ballet exams, I came home after an exam with my certificate, showing my best ever result, I had passed eighty-five points out of one hundred, I was bubbling over with excitement, waving it at Mam and asking if I could show me dad, Mam agreed but said I had to go quietly and only stay a minute, I ran down the red tiled hall and into the front room, which was now a sick room, I walked around the bottom of the bed to reach Dad's side, holding out my certificate and telling him how well I had done, he was so poorly he just pushed my hand gently away and turned his face from me - I didn't cry - but some forty years later I remembered the moment and broke my heart, crying bitterly.

I had been dancing at a garden fete in the next village, my friends and I always got the same bus home and usually because our house was close by the Butter Cross, one or two would come home with me for a while. When we got off the bus, Mr Snell came out of his shop and told me, I had to go straight home on my own and right away as Mam wanted me, I thought nothing of it just waved to my friends and skipped through the arch heading for the living room, I walked in and Mam was tearing sheets into strips and she was crying, I was frightened again, Uncle Harry was sitting in our dad's chair, everything seemed wrong, Mam held me by the shoulders and told me our dad had died, Uncle Harry took me onto his knee, I was crying miserably, unable to think or see through my tears, I was just fourteen years old, Dad was sixty-one.

There was a lady from the village in the sick room, helping Mam to - lay Dad out - Mam went to see Dad every evening before going to bed and also during the day, 'Just to make sure he was alright,' she said. We got ready for bed one night as usual when Mam said we must go and say our goodbyes to Dad, walking ahead of us up the red tiled hall, we were crying, saying we didn't want to go, she turned to us and said, 'Has your dad ever hit or hurt you?' we answered 'No,' 'Well he isn't going to hurt you now, so come along.' Our dad was lying in a coffin and there were candles burning in the room, we said our goodbyes and left the room.

He was buried in the cemetery at Tickhill Church, it didn't seem right, why couldn't' they have made room for him in the churchyard where everyone else was, the cemetery only had five or six graves, I didn't want him to be there I just wanted him to come back home. Mam hadn't stopped crying, I was frightened again and I prayed to God not to let her die too. When we went to bed that night our mam wouldn't turn the key in the door - she couldn't bear to lock him out.

CHAPTER TWENTY-FOUR
PANTOMIME / TANNER HOP

I went to my dance class as usual this particular Friday and at the end of the lesson the Miss Ashmores called me to one side. I thought I had done something wrong but I had a big surprise when they told me that if it was alright with Mam I could go into a pantomime in a proper theatre in Hartlepool, a town in the north of England, I was so excited I thought I would explode all I wanted to do was get home to tell everybody my news. Mam wasn't at all keen on the idea at first but our Kath managed to talk her round, it would also mean I would have to leave school earlier, I was due to leave after the autumn term but the rehearsals started in November. I wasn't looking forward to asking the headteacher but the Miss Ashmores wrote a letter explaining things and it was agreed that I could leave earlier - hooray.

Mam gave me a little going away party at home, the first one ever just for me - with my case packed and some money in my purse I said my goodbyes. We were all tearful especially Mam. Kath took me to Doncaster station and seeing the train approaching we hugged and hugged each other both of us crying, she put me on the train and as it pulled away I let the window down and waved and waved until she was out of sight, all of a sudden I was feeling very lonely.

When the train arrived at Hartlepool station I was met by a chaperone who took me to a boarding house on the sea front where I met the other young girls I would be working with. There were lots of rules that had to be kept, we must never go out alone, the chaperone had to be with us at all times, she took us to the theatre and brought us home, I always enjoyed the walk back along the sea front in the dark - I had never seen the sea at night, we always left the theatre before the show ended, no later than ten o'clock, we were juniors you see and that was the rule. The following day we went to the theatre to start rehearsals, it was a beautiful, big theatre much bigger than the Doncaster Grand where Kath, Millie and Margaret took us ages ago to see a pantomime - it was Babes In The Wood and I remember being frightened by the woodcutters creeping up behind the babes while they were sleeping in the woods and for many years after I would never sleep with my back to the door just in case. They also took us to see Cinderella and that was lovely especially at the end when she came down lots of stairs in her wedding dress. I loved the theatre, the smell and the atmosphere and was looking forward to the rehearsals, I couldn't wait for the day the curtains would open and I could see all the people in the seats. This pantomime was Mother Goose and we were to be the children of the old woman who lived in a shoe. Every day was exciting and different, I never got tired of dancing and singing with the orchestra playing, I was in my element I had only ever danced to the music of Mrs Ashmore playing on the piano. I wrote a long letter home every week telling Mam in detail what I was doing.

The lady we were staying with was very kind, every morning for breakfast there was a choice of milky porridge or salty, I liked the milky but I did try the salty once or twice as we never had this at home. I quite liked it, we also had toast and marmalade - I was being waited on - if Mam knew she would say 'Don't make a habit of it my girl.' The lady made lunch and supper and was always happy and smiling, of course we were there for Christmas, - my first away from home - and I was missing everyone especially our mam, she always made Christmas so special and I knew she would be missing me too. On Christmas Day the lady made a lovely turkey dinner followed by Christmas pudding - I missed the silver sixpences - there were Christmas crackers for everyone which we pulled as soon as we sat down - they had funny paper hats in them and we were all laughing as we put them on, maybe she knew we were all missing home. Her son who was a little younger than any of us gave all eight of us a present that he had made himself, he had cut eight half pennies down the middle giving one half to each of us and keeping the matching halves himself - saying that if we ever met in the future we could put them together again, what a nice present, it must have taken him a long time to cut them up.

All too soon it was over, I had actually been here for almost three months, I wrote to Mam giving her the day and time I would arrive at Doncaster station. The chaperone took us all to the station walking from one platform to another putting us on our separate trains and waving us off - I bet she was glad to see the back of us. I was eager to get home now and tell everyone how exciting it was. As the train pulled in to Doncaster station I was hanging out of the window looking frantically for a familiar face but it wasn't until I got off the train and was walking along the platform that we spotted each other - I dropped my case and ran as fast as I could straight into the arms of our Kath who was running towards me. We met with such a force that we hit our heads together, oh it was good to be back home again.

At around this time, I heard that a lady who lived on Workshop Road was a hairdresser and had started doing ladies hair at her home. One of my friends had her hair permed there and it was all lovely and curly. There was only a barber in the village where we now went for a trim so I asked me mam if I could have a perm, at first she said 'No, it would only ruin your hair.' But she gave in so off I went to get mine done. I was a bit scared when I saw the contraption that she was going to use, it looked like something out of a horror film - a tall stand with what looked like a huge upside down pan on top with electric wires dangling down and clips on the end. I was beginning to think that me mam was right and I should get off home but, it was too late for that, she had started cutting away at my hair then rolled it up in tiny little curlers really tight and every single one was pulling my hair - oh, how I hate that - then she plastered every curler with this smelly stuff, attached every one up to the electric clips that were hanging from the pan thing and switched on, well my head was getting hotter and hotter, I could hardly bear it and at last she switched it off and started taking the curlers out - what a relief. She let me see myself in the mirror, I was speechless but although I wanted to cry I said 'Lovely.' She told me not to comb it for a few days until it had settled down a bit. I didn't know how I was going to face me mam with my hair looking like this - I'd get the length of her tongue that's for sure, but as I couldn't' walk around forever I made my way home to face the music and there was a lot to face I can tell you. The following day my hair looked even worse after sleeping on it, so I had a go at combing it - no wonder I was told not to 'cos now it was all frizzy, sticking out everywhere and the more I tried the worse it got, let's face it me mam was right and I had to live with it.

The Tanner Hop - that's what they called the Friday night dance that was held in the Working Men's Institute, better known as 'The Stute' and this was the place to be on a Friday night if you were a teenager. It took us ages to get ready and as we were leaving our mam would say 'Just make sure you get the bus home.' We had to get the bus to Harworth but on Fridays we didn't get off at the picture house where our dad used to work on Saturday mornings we went to the next one, Droversdale quite a long road with houses either side, it was a five minute walk to The Stute and a three minute dash back to the bus stop after the dance. The Stute is a big, imposing building standing in its own grounds, it has one or two bars on the ground floor that we were not allowed to go into and a flight of stairs leading to the ballroom and at the top of the stairs was a lady's powder room which was always our first port of call because we didn't want to be the first ones to go in to the ballroom itself which was just along the hall so we took a long time hanging our coats, sometimes changing our shoes depending on the weather, tidying our hair and chatting to friends, we were trying to find out what boys had gone in and then first one or the other of us would peep through the powder room door whenever we heard voices, trying to keep a check on the comings and goings. We then made our entrance into the large oblong ballroom. There were chairs along the sides and a few small tables in-between, the stage at the far end was large enough for a band but we only had a man playing the latest records for us on a Friday. We always made our way across the dance floor, the girls congregating at that side, all of us sitting on the chairs giggling and nudging each other pretending to be enjoying ourselves and the boys on the other side looking mean and moody. It was always the girls that got on to the dance floor first once we had sorted out a partner - not a boy just one of our friends - trouble was we could never agree who was going to lead - you know take the boy's part - I couldn't lead, I got muddled up but our Doreen could so I grabbed her before one of her friends did, then we would show off - well we could 'cos we had good teachers didn't we? Time and again us girls danced together and by the time the boys joined us it was nearly time to go home. I think we all dreaded being asked and if we saw one looking then walking over to us we looked away and pretended we hadn't noticed especially if we had an eye for someone else but rather than sit on the sidelines we danced with them and if truth be known enjoyed every dance. The last bus to Tickhill left Bircotes at eleven fifteen and the dance finished at eleven o'clock but nobody wanted to miss the last waltz nor did we want it to end so by the time we got our coats and with some of the boys hoping for a goodnight kiss we all made a mad dash to the bus stop. We didn't always get there on time and had to walk home, some of the boys would walk part way with us but we still had to walk along the dark Harworth Road, into Spital and passing The Gas House where we used to live before seeing any street lights then all the way up Sunderland Street to the Butter Cross only to get told off by our mam for missing the bus.

One Friday our Enid went with her friend and they missed the bus and started to walk home and half way along the Harworth Road they saw the headlights of a car and as her friend's dad was one of the few people in Tickhill that owned a car guessed it must be him and it was, and he was mad, he bundled them both in and headed for home. They lived at the bottom of Sunderland Street and that is where he stopped telling his daughter to get indoors and our Enid to get off home, so all alone late at night our Enid belted up Sunderland Street as fast as her legs would carry her, straight through the arch like a bat out of hell not daring to tell our mam what had happened in case she got a wallop.

By the way I must just tell you - we did go to the library with no books whenever they held an old-fashioned dance night - and I got to dance the old-fashioned waltz - magic.

I still went to my dance classes when I came home from Hartlepool and got a job in Bawtry - a little market town on the Great North Road, the focal point is The Crown Hotel that is reported to have been built on three shires - Bawtry is about four miles from Tickhill. If I cycled, which I did more often than not as the bus from Tickhill went to Harworth and through Bircotes before it eventually arrived at Bawtry which took for ever, where as to go on the bike I went down Sunderland Street to the cross-roads at Spital and up Spital Hill on the long, straight road to Bawtry but I soon had to get off and push the bike up the hill - as I've said before Spital Hill is blinking steep and coming home you needed a good set of brakes in order to ride down and but for the cross-roads at the bottom the speed you gathered on the way down would have got you all the way to the Butter Cross - well almost. I was going to work in a little coffee bar that had just opened opposite The Crown Hotel, our Enid went there as well to look after the lady's two little girls - well she was a dab hand at that, she'd had plenty of practice! One of my friends from dance class lived in Bawtry just along from The Crown and I sometimes called to see her, her mam had a dry cleaning shop and quite often when I called her mam would be in the back room with a great pile of men's trousers brushing the fluff out of the turn-ups, checking for lose buttons and dipping her hand into the pockets making sure they were empty before putting them into separate piles for cleaning and I was so glad I wasn't going to work in a dry cleaner's shop.

The coffee bar was bright and sunny, it was only small, the high counter went from the large window facing the street to the kitchen door at the back and had bar stools along the front and a few small tables and chairs dotted around behind. We served frothy coffee, milkshakes, knickerbocker glories and ice cream sundaes, there were cakes and chocolates and sandwiches were made to order in the kitchen, plus

Welsh rarebit - I liked making this and I liked eating it an all, 'cos our mam didn't have a big electric toaster or a grill, well she couldn't, don't forget we only had one electric plug in our house and we could hardly stand a toaster in the little window.

It was while I was working here that the Miss Ashmores put me in touch with a lady in Rotherham - an industrial town about seven miles outside Tickhill - she had contacts in London who would be able to take me to auditions and I needed to go to London if I wanted to dance and oh I wanted to dance on a stage. I went to Rotherham once a week and was taught more dance steps and deportment, I had photographs taken to be sent to London and over the weeks she arranged for me to visit her friends. I enjoyed working in the coffee bar but was getting restless and wanted to be off, the few times I had mentioned it to me mam she said things like - 'We'll see when you get a bit older.' One evening me and our Kath were going to the pictures in Harworth. I must have been dragging my heels as we walked to the bus stop, she looked at me and said 'Where's your smile?' and through my tears I told her everything was in place for me to go to London but I hadn't told mam yet 'cos 'I know she won't let me go even though I probably won't be gone long because I'll miss you all and be too home-sick to stay away but - I just had to try.' She calmed me down and told me to leave everything to her and she would talk our mam round 'So dry your eyes, jump on the bus and let's enjoy the pictures.' - My smile was back again, my big sister could do it every time.

It didn't take long for our Kath to talk Mam round, I now had the name and address of the people I was going to stay with and a letter of introduction. Mam was going through my clothes making sure I had everything I needed and I had been putting some money away every week ready for the day. Mam didn't want me to go by train, so she mentioned my going to a coach driver, Mam used to get coach trips up to go to the seaside and knew the coach driver very well, he said he would be going to London and would call for me and so with my case packed and feeling just a little frightened I said my goodbyes and left Tickhill - my childhood over!